I0824878

ZARDU LAYAK: THE CRIMSON APOSTLE

BOOK 1 – HORUS RISING
Dan Abnett

BOOK 2 – FALSE GODS
Graham McNeill

BOOK 3 – GALAXY IN FLAMES
Ben Counter

BOOK 4 – THE FLIGHT OF THE EISENSTEIN
James Swallow

BOOK 5 – FULGRIM
Graham McNeill

BOOK 6 – DESCENT OF ANGELS
Mitchel Scanlon

BOOK 7 – LEGION
Dan Abnett

BOOK 8 – BATTLE FOR THE ABYSS
Ben Counter

BOOK 9 – MECHANICUM
Graham McNeill

BOOK 10 – TALES OF HERESY
edited by Nick Kyme and Lindsey Priestley

BOOK 11 – FALLEN ANGELS
Mike Lee

BOOK 12 – A THOUSAND SONS
Graham McNeill

BOOK 13 – NEMESIS
James Swallow

BOOK 14 – THE FIRST HERETIC
Aaron Dembski-Bowden

BOOK 15 – PROSPERO BURNS
Dan Abnett

BOOK 16 – AGE OF DARKNESS
edited by Christian Dunn

BOOK 17 – THE OUTCAST DEAD
Graham McNeill

BOOK 18 – DELIVERANCE LOST
Gav Thorpe

BOOK 19 – KNOW NO FEAR
Dan Abnett

BOOK 20 – THE PRIMARCHS
edited by Christian Dunn

BOOK 21 – FEAR TO TREAD
James Swallow

BOOK 22 – SHADOWS OF TREACHERY
edited by Christian Dunn and Nick Kyme

BOOK 23 – ANGEL EXTERMINATUS
Graham McNeill

BOOK 24 – BETRAYER
Aaron Dembski-Bowden

BOOK 25 – MARK OF CALTH
edited by Laurie Goulding

BOOK 26 – VULKAN LIVES
Nick Kyme

BOOK 27 – THE UNREMEMBERED EMPIRE
Dan Abnett

BOOK 28 – SCARS
Chris Wraight

BOOK 29 – VENGEFUL SPIRIT
Graham McNeill

BOOK 30 – THE DAMNATION OF PYTHOS
David Annandale

BOOK 31 – LEGACIES OF BETRAYAL
edited by Laurie Goulding

BOOK 32 – DEATHFIRE
Nick Kyme

BOOK 33 – WAR WITHOUT END
edited by Laurie Goulding

BOOK 34 – PHAROS
Guy Haley

BOOK 35 – EYE OF TERRA
edited by Laurie Goulding

BOOK 36 – THE PATH OF HEAVEN
Chris Wraight

BOOK 37 – THE SILENT WAR
edited by Laurie Goulding

BOOK 38 – ANGELS OF CALIBAN
Gav Thorpe

BOOK 39 – PRAETORIAN OF DORN
John French

BOOK 40 – CORAX
Gav Thorpe

BOOK 41 – THE MASTER OF MANKIND
Aaron Dembski-Bowden

BOOK 42 – GARRO
James Swallow

BOOK 43 – SHATTERED LEGIONS
edited by Laurie Goulding

BOOK 44 – THE CRIMSON KING
Graham McNeill

BOOK 45 – TALLARN
John French

BOOK 46 – RUINSTORM
David Annandale

BOOK 47 – OLD EARTH
Nick Kyme

BOOK 48 – THE BURDEN OF LOYALTY
edited by Laurie Goulding

BOOK 49 – WOLFSBANE
Guy Haley

BOOK 50 – BORN OF FLAME
Nick Kyme

BOOK 51 – SLAVES TO DARKNESS
John French

BOOK 52 – HERALDS OF THE SIEGE
edited by Nick Kyme and
Laurie Goulding

BOOK 53 – TITANDEATH
Guy Haley

BOOK 54 – THE BURIED DAGGER
James Swallow

THE HORUS HERESY®
SIEGE OF TERRA

BOOK 1 – THE SOLAR WAR
John French

BOOK 2 – THE LOST AND THE DAMNED
Guy Haley

BOOK 3 – THE FIRST WALL
Gav Thorpe

BOOK 4 – SATURNINE
Dan Abnett

BOOK 5 – MORTIS
John French

BOOK 6 – WARHAWK
Chris Wraight

BOOK 7 – ECHOES OF ETERNITY
Aaron Dembski-Bowden

BOOK 8 – THE END AND THE DEATH:
VOLUME I
VOLUME II
VOLUME III
Dan Abnett

ERA OF RUIN (ANTHOLOGY)
Dan Abnett, Aaron Dembski-Bowden,
John French, Guy Haley, Nick Kyme,
Gav Thorpe and Chris Wraight

SONS OF THE SELENAR (NOVELLA)
Graham McNeill

FURY OF MAGNUS (NOVELLA)
Graham McNeill

GARRO: KNIGHT OF GREY (NOVELLA)
James Swallow

The Horus Heresy Character Series

VALDOR: BIRTH OF THE IMPERIUM
Chris Wraight

LUTHER: FIRST OF THE FALLEN
Gav Thorpe

SIGISMUND: THE ETERNAL CRUSADER
John French

EIDOLON: THE AURIC HAMMER
Marc Collins

ZARDU LAYAK: THE CRIMSON APOSTLE
Rich McCormick

ZARDU LAYAK: THE CRIMSON APOSTLE

RICH McCORMICK

BLACK LIBRARY

A BLACK LIBRARY PUBLICATION

First published in 2026.
This edition published in 2026 by
Black Library, Games Workshop Ltd., Willow Road,
Nottingham, NG7 2WS, UK.
Represented by: Games Workshop Limited – Irish branch,
Unit 3, Lower Liffey Street, Dublin 1,
D01 K199, Ireland.

10 9 8 7 6 5 4 3 2 1

Produced by Games Workshop in Nottingham.
Cover illustration by Daniel Batista.

A CIP record for this book is available from the British Library.

ISBN 13: 978-1-83609-301-5

Printed and bound in China.

For Finn.

It is a time of legend.

Mighty heroes battle for the right to rule the galaxy. The vast armies of the Emperor of Mankind conquer the stars in a Great Crusade – the myriad alien races are to be smashed by His elite warriors and wiped from the face of history.

The dawn of a new age of supremacy for humanity beckons. Gleaming citadels of marble and gold celebrate the many victories of the Emperor, as system after system is brought back under His control. Triumphs are raised on a million worlds to record the epic deeds of His most powerful champions.

First and foremost amongst these are the primarchs, superhuman beings who have led the Space Marine Legions in campaign after campaign. They are unstoppable and magnificent, the pinnacle of the Emperor's genetic experimentation, while the Space Marines themselves are the mightiest human warriors the galaxy has ever known, each capable of besting a hundred normal men or more in combat.

Many are the tales told of these legendary beings. From the halls of the Imperial Palace on Terra to the outermost reaches of Ultima Segmentum, their deeds are known to be shaping the very future of the galaxy. But can such souls remain free of doubt and corruption forever? Or will the temptation of greater power prove too much for even the most loyal sons of the Emperor?

The seeds of heresy have already been sown, and the start of the greatest war in the history of mankind is but a few years away…

PROLOGUE

When the dreams first came, Zardu Layak did not sleep often. None of his kind did; their genetically enhanced bodies and brains reduced the need for rest. But while his brothers sometimes set aside their toil and drifted willingly into slumber, he did not. He worked in the practice cages until sweat covered every inch of his body. He worked until he could fight no longer, until his body was thrumming with exhaustion, his blade-sharp mind finally dulled.

He fought sleep because he knew what waited on the other side.

It had been there since Monarchia.

Monarchia – the great dividing line. The eclipse of his Legion. The sun had set. It would not rise again.

And so, after he could fight it no longer, he gave in to the darkness.

Slowly, it curdled, turning to light again. At first it was weak, but it grew stronger, until it was blinding. Not sunlight, but something brighter and colder – so bright that it shone through the meat and muscle of his hands, casting the bones within as shadows. He squeezed his eyes shut, but still he could see it, burning pain on his optic nerves. They acclimatised, achingly slow, until finally he could make out a figure at the centre of the light.

It was massive. Luminous, in all senses, and even though he could not make out its features, he knew it was both glorious and terrible to behold.

It always waited for him, here.

It called to him.

'My son.'

Layak was strong and quick, a living weapon created in Terra's genetic forges. He had fought a thousand battles for his Legion. He was a captain, a leader of the great Ashen Circle, and he had burned hundreds of worlds. But he was a child once more in the figure's presence. Small and weak, pathetic against such majesty.

'Father,' he said, a quaver in his voice.

The figure turned, and he saw Lorgar's face. Intricate lines of script marked the primarch's bronze skin, blessings and invocations tracing his high cheekbones and across his shaven scalp, disappearing beneath his stone-grey armour. They seemed to swim in the searing light. They were still beyond Layak's understanding, then.

'Come with me,' Lorgar said, and took his hand. The light faded, becoming weak and grey, and suddenly they stood amongst the ruins of Monarchia, where his Legion had been castigated at the hands of the Emperor and the Ultramarines.

It had been beautiful, once. A city of temples and churches, of peace and worship, before it had been razed to the ground for the sin of belief. Now it was a wound on the world, a scar that would not heal. The ash still hung in the air. Even in a dream, he could taste it, greasy and bitter.

The figure spoke with Lorgar's voice, clear and resonant, but his words were weighed down with a sadness that even Layak's transhuman mind could not comprehend. Such sadness that he thought that his chest would collapse in on itself like a black hole, falling towards a single point in history.

'I must ask something of you,' Lorgar said.

He rejected his father at first. He closed his eyes and blocked his ears, not trusting the apparition in his dreams. Monarchia had broken so many of his brothers. Some had been consumed by fury, their souls burnt out in the flame of failure. Others were too dejected to fight on – as beings of faith, they simply failed to function after being spurned so viscerally by the very god they worshipped. And so, when he began to be visited by the ghost of his father in dreams so real that he could taste the failure of his Legion's past, he thought only that his time had come, that he too was broken. He had always been known as a rational man – something of a rarity amongst a Legion of zealots – and he had rationalised this, too.

'I understand why I am here,' he said, as he stared across a dream of the desolate city. Dunes of ash rose against a grey horizon.

Lorgar listened, patiently awaiting his truth.

'I am mad,' Layak said plainly.

His father laughed in response. It was an impossible sound. It moved through the registers, reaching across time and space, terrifyingly cruel, and suffocatingly kind. Golden eyes looked down. They were hard, but not harsh, like the carved topaz of a long-forgotten civilisation.

'I thought I was mad, once. After Monarchia, when my own father spurned my worship, when he laid my children low, for the sin of belief. I thought that there was a rot, deep in my soul. A flaw.' Lorgar placed a hand to his chest, and his golden eyes filled with tears. 'I gave penance. I exiled myself, and during my long pilgrimage, I discovered the truth.

'You are not mad, my child, no more so than any of your number. The gods are real. The only madness is to deny them. To stand against them.'

A glimmer of hope rose in Layak's hearts, and as if in symphony with the sensation, the sun of the planet Khur broke the horizon.

'You have discovered the same truth that I did amongst the stars,' Lorgar told him. 'There is madness at the core of existence – and you have stood in its face, unafraid and unbowed. I appear to you not because you are broken, but because you are chosen.'

The word seemed to stop time itself. Ash hung in the air, and Layak's chest felt heavy, as if his hearts struggled to pump his own blood.

'Chosen?' Layak managed, turning to face the figure of his father. He was a child against the giant. Lorgar's cloak rippled in the ash-laden wind, rendering his form indistinct, inconsistent. Like a ghost. Layak could not see the details of his face – Lorgar's shaven head blocked Khur's newly risen sun, casting him in a halo of white light. Only gold eyes remained.

'Chosen,' Lorgar said. 'You have a purpose, my son. Are you ready to accept it?'

Layak felt shame loosen its grip on his body, its cold fingers releasing one by one.

Chosen.

'I am,' Zardu Layak said, and the dream of Monarchia drifted away like ash on the wind.

It was replaced in an instant by a landscape of frozen taiga. Trees stretched into the midnight sky, casting ink-black shadows across the dark earth. The air carried the sound of chanting, and the shadows writhed to their song.

Layak's armour was stone grey in the blackness of the night. Lorgar spoke from the frigid night air, the primarch's body somewhere beyond vision.

'You have borne the holy fire of my Ashen Circle, child. You have burned the galaxy in my name. In the Emperor's name.'

Layak touched the symbol carved in his breastplate without thought, tracing the edges of the flame motif.

'But I have a new purpose for you. One that will determine the future of our Legion.' Lorgar's golden eyes seemed to flicker, a whorl of colour in their depths. 'A purpose that will determine the future of this galaxy.'

He took Layak's chin between his thumb and forefinger, as if appraising him. The digits were massive, but the touch was gentle. He felt lighter than he had in decades.

'I will do as you ask,' Layak said.

'You are brave,' Lorgar replied. His smile filled Layak's body with light, bright and golden. 'But you are not ready to face your true purpose yet. For now, I ask no more of you than I have of myself. Please, child, search for truth. I fought for my father, I killed for my father, I burned the galaxy for my father. A righteous cause, I thought. But...' Lorgar sighed. 'All I wanted was truth, child. I thought I had found it in the Emperor, but I see now that I was deceived. And so, I have found my own truth. I did not find it in one place, but many. I ask the same of you. The scraps of truth that you find – do not burn them. Save them. Protect them. Learn from them. And then, you may come to understand the universe as I have come to understand it.'

'But that... that is betrayal...'

'Yes,' Lorgar said. 'The first of many.'

From the spire, the warrior saw the sweep of the underhive laid out before him, separated only by a thin layer of armaglass. There were a million lives in its depths. A million dreams, a million fears, a million beliefs. From up here, they were nothing. So small as to be invisible.

To be one of those little lives, he thought. He felt emotion swell in his body, pinpricks of feeling raising the hairs on his muscled arms. Pity, or revulsion, he could not determine. Two faces of the same coin.

What a waste of life, all those little people. Their attention on the mundanities of existence, when something so much greater was so close. All they needed to do was look up. Up, beyond the spire of metal and glass. Up, to the heavens.

The priest lay slumped against that glass. His robes had been red, once, the colour of healthy blood. Now they were mud brown and pus yellow, the colours of squalor. His dark eyes were rimed with some sickness.

'Please…' the priest begged. His voice was like discarded snake-skin – paper-thin, dry as desert sand. 'Please, spare me.'

The request tugged at the corner of the warrior's mouth, and he reached up and unclasped his helmet to let the smile free. He slid the modified Mark II helm from his head, and tasted the air. Sour and sweet, like a gangrenous wound. He met the priest's gaze with his own eyes – light brown, flecked with gold – and slowly, carefully, laid down his axe-rake on the carpeted floor.

He gestured to the man's stomach. The movement made the priest wince. Something moved under his robes.

'Show me,' the warrior said simply.

'No!' The priest moaned, and twisted away, as if he was trying to escape through the thick glass. He cradled his arms over his swollen abdomen, a protective gesture. The warrior stepped closer, and cocked his head to the side.

'Show me,' he said. 'I will not ask again.'

'Please, leave me alone,' the priest whimpered.

The warrior laughed, not unkindly.

'I cannot do that,' he said. He touched his knee, pointing two fingers to the flame motif that rose from his armour. It was copper gold on stone grey, dulled by age and by flame. 'Do you see this? This means that I am of the Ashen Circle,' he said. The priest looked up, rheumy eyes wet with tears. He did not understand.

The warrior continued. 'We are destroyers. We burn libraries and tear down temples, cleansing the galaxy of falsehoods, in the name of our father, and the master he serves. When the Ashen Circle descend, none escape judgement. But,' he said, smiling warmly, 'I will make sure that you escape agony. All you need do is co-operate.' He beckoned to the man, his palm open, inviting. 'Come now. Give it to me. I promise that I will make it quick.'

The priest hissed, half-laugh, half in pain. 'Cannot escape… agony,' he said. 'Must embrace it. Become it. It is… truth.'

Some wisdom from this creature. This prize may have been worth the effort, the warrior thought. The deceit, the misdirection, the stain on his honour, and what remained of his soul. All may have been worth the price. It was too late. He would find out, either way.

'You understand as I do,' the warrior said, his smile fading. He brought his helmet once more over his face, and his gold-flecked eyes were gone, hidden now by a single-slit visor of blood red. It locked the priest with an unblinking gaze as the warrior continued, his voice now drained of its warmth in its vox amplification. 'Mercy is a failing.'

The priest opened bleeding lips to speak, but it was too late. The warrior was upon him, lifting him into the air, holding him suspended with a single arm. With the other, he pulled apart the priest's ragged robes to reveal the body beneath, and the reason for his arrival on this world.

There was a book in the man's belly. Sick flesh grew around it, the skin weeping and inflamed where it touched leather and parchment. The cover was inlaid with shapes – circles that seemed to turn forever, drawing life and breath from those who lost themselves in their cycle.

The warrior expected more pleas for mercy, but the priest was convulsing in his grip, his emaciated body shuddering and shaking. He was twice the priest's height and many orders of magnitude his strength, but the warrior struggled to hold the robed man as he contorted, his frail body given unholy strength. His jaw fell open, and the warrior smelt reeking breath, hot and foul – the scent of pestilence assaulting the warrior's senses even beneath his helmet. The priest was laughing, the warrior realised – a hacking, retching sound that sent his eyes rolling in his skull.

Words fell out as he laughed. 'This is the only truth,' the priest said, his voice now deep and timbrous. The words repeated, from the walls, from the armaglass, until the convulsions stopped, and the priest met the warrior's cyclopean stare. A flicker of recognition crossed his cataracted eyes.

The priest began to chant, words that the warrior knew were to be found within the pages of the book in the man's belly. They were ancient, and not words in the sense that mortals would understand them. They twisted in the air, searching for warmth like worms, before finding it. The warrior felt their effects in his own body as they pulled at blood and bone, shaping them to accept disease and degradation. His hearts slowed and his blood thickened, trying to clot in his arteries. Strong as they were, even his muscles slackened, and the priest dropped from his hands.

The robed figure rose to his feet without effort, lifted as if on strings as a child would raise a marionette. 'Give in,' the priest said, in words older than human civilisation. His feet lifted from the ground as the warrior fell to his knees. The book juddered in his stomach, pus bubbling from its pages. 'Give yourself to decay. Accept your weakness.'

The words stoked a light in the warrior's hearts, bright, like the flame that signified his order. He shielded it, that heat and light, letting it grow in size, letting it burn the rot that was settling in his transhuman body.

His blood quickened, and his muscles strengthened. His senses returned, and he heard the million voices from below, in all their chaos. He raised his slit helm to meet the gaze of the priest.

'A fine trick,' the warrior said. 'But I am destined for more.'

He willed his hearts to beat, forcing hot blood through his veins and arteries. Standing now, he towered over the priest, and with his voice – amplified by technology and the gifts of the warp – he recited his own words. The words of his father, and of his acolytes and aides. Words he had inscribed on his own body. They had changed him already, just as he had been promised, in so many glorious ways.

He stood above the curve of the underhive, with its millions of little lives, and his hearts beat to the rhythm of the cosmos.

The priest stared, his jaw slack, his body frail once more. His words ceased. They had no power over the warrior.

'How… how did you do that?' he breathed, so weak as to be almost inaudible.

'I am also a seeker of truth,' the warrior said. He retrieved his axe-rake, and set about his work.

It was small. That was good. Other artefacts had been larger things, difficult to conceal from his brothers. He wiped mucus and blood from the dark leather of the book's cover. Geometric shapes revealed themselves, throbbing on the book's surface. He let his eyes linger on them as his mind travelled their lengths towards conclusions not yet seen.

Below him, the priest gurgled. Somehow, despite his injuries, he marshalled the strength to speak.

'What…' he began, then coughed wetly. 'What will you do with it?'

The warrior lifted his eyes from the book, and tucked it behind his slate-grey breastplate.

'I will read it,' he said. He could not tell his brothers, but he could be honest to this doomed creature. This priest had brought this gift to him. He owed him that much. 'Maybe I will find more truth amongst its pages.'

'And me?' the priest asked.

'You were right. You cannot escape agony.'

The warrior raised his flamer and squeezed the trigger. A gout of flame roared from under his armoured wrist, and the priest – and the view of the underhive behind him – was consumed by fire.

'My purge is complete,' the warrior lied to his brothers. He felt the book throbbing gently against his chest.

'All is ash. Nothing remains.'

Years passed, and the Legion changed. Slowly, at first, and then all at once, as Lorgar's new religion found root in the empty hearts of the XVII. Zardu Layak took his name mere weeks before the Word Bearers' betrayal was laid bare by the massacre at Isstvan V, its meaning apt for one with such a collection of occult knowledge – the Eater of Wisdom.

By this time, the thing that visited him in the night had changed. It still wore Lorgar's form, but it spoke with different voices, and it knew things that even Lorgar could not.

He had done as it had asked anyway. Shame had prickled at his body as he had lied to his brothers the first time, but the betrayals of their trust came easier to him with each curio smuggled from a world, each arcane treatise added to his collection. He had built a hoard of such objects – as profane as they were powerful – in defiance of his orders, of his very purpose as an anointed member of the Ashen Circle.

And in return, it had rewarded him.

It had given him strength. His body had been altered, further still than his kin. The changes were subtle, but he felt them as they manifested: in his skin, which burned with the words inlaid into it; in his hearts, which thumped to a rhythm that he heard in the depths of the void. Yet more secrets that he kept from his brothers.

It had given him knowledge. He studied the words of Lorgar and of Erebus again and again, re-reading passages already seared into his eidetic memory and etched into his skin, and found that he could understand them in a new light. He saw the Primordial Truth as his father had – the darkness at the core of the galaxy. He learned how to weave the warp to his will, how to wield the powers of sorcery, shaping flesh and blood, creating life, and sowing death.

Most of all, it had given him purpose. Once, he had been an iconoclast, the fiery vengeance of a false god. Now, he atoned for his mistakes, protecting the truth – the Primordial Truth – from destruction.

His boons had not come without pain. He had rejected his oaths, both to his Legion and to the Ashen Circle. He had lied to his brothers, even killed them, when they had uncovered his subterfuge. Even with the Word Bearers in open rebellion, with worship of the Pantheon ubiquitous amongst members of the Legion, Layak could not risk his work being uncovered, or his collection falling into the wrong hands. The outbreak of Horus' rebellion had only elevated this risk, the splintering of the established order leaving space for ambitious men to usurp him.

He was not at Isstvan V, but he remained busy, expanding his mastery of the sorcerous arts and building a network of acolytes and believers who would help him rise through the ranks of the Word Bearers, and to fulfil his purpose. He was ready, as he told Lorgar when the two figures stood together in a dream years after the first, once more looking across the grave of Monarchia.

'I have learned much,' Layak said. He raised his hand, palm to the heavens. With a soft slicing sound, the skin of his palm split open like a flower, eight petals of flesh peeling back to reveal raw muscle beneath. Even in the dream, the pain was real, and it brought clarity. Layak focused on the blood bubbling from his flayed hand, and brought more from his veins and vessels, shaping it as it rose into Monarchia's still air. An eight-pointed star hung above his palm, beautiful in its brutality.

'I have mastered blood sorcery. I have bound creatures of the warp to my will. I have shackled souls, turning them to my purpose.'

'And yet, there is much more that you do not yet know.'

Layak let his concentration lapse, and the star of blood lost its shape and splashed to the earth below, darkness on darkness.

'I know that you are not my father,' he countered.

Lorgar bristled.

'You wear his skin, you speak with his voice, but you are not Lorgar.'

A cold wind rose from the dead earth, flakes of black ash lifting in the updraught. Lorgar turned on his son, his sudden anger terrible to behold

'You deny me?' the figure of the Word Bearers' primarch asked, his face and voice both thunder.

Layak took a step to steady himself against the growing gale, but did not back down. He met Lorgar's rage with an absence of emotion. He had rationalised this as well. 'No. You have given me all I have asked for, and more. You may not be my father, but as long as I serve you, then I believe that he and I serve the same master.'

The wind faded in an instant, the flakes of ash fell, and Lorgar's face became placid again.

'You are perceptive,' he said. 'But you must be strong enough to walk your path alone.'

'With your gifts, I am already strong.'

Lorgar offered a father's knowing chuckle, and placed a finger against Layak's breastbone. It seemed to phase through his slate-grey armour, resting against the skin beneath.

'I know you, child. There has always been a void at your core, deeper and darker than any of your brothers. A void carved by a life of such perfect misery, such loneliness, such pain…'

Layak saw himself as a child on a derelict orbital, weeping amongst a mountain of corpses. He saw his human body racked with agony, changed beyond understanding against his will. He saw the symbol of his Legion – the Perfect City – razed to the ground by order of the being he worshipped. A being who rejected that worship and, inadvertently, exposed the terrible truth at the core of reality.

The truth, once he understood it, became Layak's own. The agony, the misery – they were not random. They were by design. The Emperor had lied. Gods existed, and they gorged themselves on human suffering. Pain was the natural order of the galaxy, and to reject that truth, to fight against ruin – that was true madness.

'I see it,' Lorgar said. 'I feel it, belief as thick as the blood that pumps in your veins. Belief is all you have. It was your belief that brought you to my attention.'

Lorgar sighed, and Layak's chest ached at the sound, so hard-wired into his body was his desire to please his gene-father.

'But still,' the primarch said, tapping Layak's chest, 'too much of the man remains.'

'I will destroy him. Grant me more boons. Make me stronger still, and I will bring your truth – the only truth – to the galaxy.'

'Any warrior can become powerful. But you must become something more. Something *pure*.'

'Then tell me how,' Layak said, his patience burning away. 'You have promised me purpose. What is it?'

The words hung in the silence of the dead air, and Layak thought he had gone too far. He braced himself for rebuke. The Lorgar of his dreams played the role of his father expertly, and sons rarely spoke to their primarchs so without punishment. But Lorgar was still, his only movement a slow smile creeping across his tattooed face.

'Perhaps it is time,' he said. 'I will show you where your path leads.' He turned to the horizon. 'Come with me,' he said, 'and I will show you your future.'

Monarchia disappeared once more, and Layak stood in another city. One he did not recognise. It was not a city, in truth – that was too small a word for it. A fortress, instead, like a castle of old, but at a scale he had never seen before. A mountain blasted flat, its vast plateau home to a billion souls. He stood amongst those souls, amidst the chaos and dust of a makeshift market. Humans in rags pushed past him, carrying strange fruits, swaddled babies, barking canines, and other animals. Voices were raised, words were exchanged, blades were flashed. Lives were bartered for food, for coin, for favours, and for knowledge. It was just one of ten thousand such places in this city, one of millions on this world. Not just any world – this was the crucible of humanity. Terra. Even in the shadow of the monument to this world's false god, the petty business of survival continued.

The sheer weight of it hit Layak like a slug to the stomach, almost taking his breath away. Generations of pain, of misery, of emotions spilled like blood. It was layered into the very bedrock of this decapitated mountain like fossil deposits.

'You can taste it.'

Lorgar stood in the market, amongst but somehow apart from the mass of humanity. Hunched people moved around him, a rock in the stream.

Layak realised he had been holding his breath, and sucked a lungful of the city's air. It was thick with the stench of humanity.

'Why am I here?' he asked.

'Because it will be here. This is where you, my son, will open the way. This is your purpose. You will show these benighted souls truth. You will become its vessel.'

A light shone on the market. The humans stopped in their tracks, raising their arms to shield their eyes. Some ran. Some simply stood, jaws slack, eyes wide, awe clear on their faces. The light was golden, but – he realised – it was not the sun. It came from him.

His chest swelled with the brightness, liquid gold coursing from his hearts, through his arteries and veins like blood. It reached his fingers and his toes, such a suffusion that he felt it in his throat like a scream, waiting to be let out. He opened his mouth, and he was racked with pain. It was pure, cleansing, an agony so intense that he forgot the misery around him, forgot the shame of Monarchia, forgot the void at his own core. A beam of light rose from his throat, punching through the clouds above to the sky beyond. The light grew, until even his body with its enhancements could hold it no longer, and the market was consumed in glory.

And then the light faded, and he returned to the ruins of Monarchia, choking. Lorgar stood over him as he fell to his knees, spitting fizzing saliva into the ashes of countless dead.

'Terra…' Layak said, when he could breathe again.

'Yes, my child. You are to be the beginning of the end.'

'How… how do I become what I am destined to be?'

Lorgar smiled.

'Too much of you remains. Too much of your humanity. Too much of your… weakness. Mercy. Doubt. Loyalty.' He shook his head, and Layak felt the waves of sadness radiate off his father like engine wash. The primarch moved differently now. Great shoulders were hunched under etched ceramite pauldrons too narrow to contain them, and his voice echoed, as though many were speaking.

'I will burn it from my soul. I will do whatever it takes.'

'I have faith in you, child.'

Layak found himself standing before a gate. It was built from sandstone, its surface marked with shapes. Their edges had been softened by epochs, but the lines still ran deep and clear. Layak recognised some of them from the texts in his collection, but not all. There was still so much to learn.

His hearts beat hard in his chest.

Beyond the gate was darkness, swirling and thick, and inside the darkness, he saw three figures. They were tall, like him, and as he focused on the void of their faces, he saw eyes open. Flecked with gold. They each held a blade – curved, cruel, and thrumming with power.

'The Anakatis,' Lorgar said. 'Ancient weapons, imbued with power. Your brothers have claimed them. Brothers closest to you of all.'

Hebek.

Kulnar.

Saucan.

Each one a part of his past. A part of his soul.

The darkness split open. Beyond, Layak saw a mountain, rising tall and silent against a white sky.

'What is it?' Layak asked.

'A grave,' Lorgar said.

'What would you have me do?'

'Find your brothers. Take the blades, and then, at the base of the mountain, cleanse yourself, so that you can become the vessel foretold.'

Lorgar tilted Layak's face towards his own.

'This is your purpose, child,' he said.

PART ONE

MISERICORDIA

CHAPTER ONE

It was the smell. Yergorin Barnhart had become accustomed to a lot of strange things during her time in service of the Word Bearers, but no matter how hard she tried to block it out, she couldn't ignore the smell. It hung in the air of the muster hall, thick and rancid, like copper and decaying things, strong enough that even the musty scent of one hundred soldiers in unwashed robes could not overpower it.

Barnhart turned from the troops, and, with a surreptitious motion, smeared two lines of incense oil under her nostrils. It didn't mask the stench entirely, but it was better than nothing.

'Don't let them see you do that,' Jassim said from behind her. Barnhart started, almost dropping the vial of scented oil.

'Commander, I didn't...'

'It shows weakness, lieutenant. If you are to lead these people, then you must appear strong. Even if you aren't.'

Jassim stepped from the darkness at the edge of the hall. He was a large man, but he had an uncanny ability to move silently, appearing where his officers and soldiers least expected. Wild rumours swirled amongst the junior ranks of the Children of the Blessed Moon – some even said that the commander had found something during one forgotten planetfall that let him trade places with his own shadow. Jassim did nothing to quash the rumours, more than happy to let himself be mythologised amongst the superstitious Children of the Blessed Moon.

'Yes, sir,' Barnhart said. 'Understood, sir.' She wiped at her top lip, making a show of smearing the oil from her face without trying too hard to remove the sweet-smelling unguent. Jassim waited with a hesitancy that Barnhart found peculiar. 'Was there anything else, sir?' she asked.

'Yes, lieutenant. Yes, there was.' He paused, and she swore she saw a touch of fear in his leathery features. 'I have been summoned. I would like you to accompany me.'

'Of course, sir. Where are we going?'

'To meet with one of our lords,' Jassim said.

'The Word Bearers, sir?'

'Correct.'

A small shiver ran through Barnhart's body.

Decades in service meant that she was numb to the realities of war: the strained cries of the dying, calling for their mothers or their lovers as the entrails slid from their ruined bodies; the bitter thrill of killing, the acrid taste on the back of the tongue as another body slumped to the dirt.

But what the Word Bearers did was beyond war. On battlefields she had shared with the XVII Legion, Barnhart had seen pyres of the still-living put to the torch in the name of Horus and his righteous rebellion, their screams loud enough to tear the very sky apart. She had heard worse from other soldiers, stories shared in hushed tones in mess halls by haunted figures of already compliant populations rounded up and sacrificed in the name of new gods. They had been cleansed for days beforehand, washed and fed, they had said, before warriors of the XVII, stripped to the waist and armed only with long blades, descended upon them. At sunrise, not a mortal remained alive.

'Lieutenant?' Jassim asked. Barnhart shook the shiver away, and fell in behind her commanding officer as they strode from the muster hall, the stench of dead things still burning her senses.

'Who is he?' Barnhart asked as she walked the halls of the battleship *Unwilling Sacrifice* with her commanding officer. Glow-globes offered their quivering light from alcoves, barely illuminating the pair's path, leaving stained shadows on the walls.

'His name is Zardu Layak,' Jassim said. 'A captain of the Ashen Circle, one of the Legion's finest, feted by his brothers, and anointed by greater powers.'

'And why would he want to speak with you?'

Jassim's head snapped to regard her, his weathered face hard, his pride pricked.

'The Children are a brave unit with a grand history, of course,' she added, mollifying the older man. 'But our orders have come from above, not the Adeptus Astartes themselves. What does he want with us?'

He turned his head back to the dimly lit corridor, and breathed deeply.

'The galaxy has changed since Isstvan V,' Jassim said. 'We are arrayed against our brothers and sisters now, a holy war against the false Emperor's corrupt empire. The old structures are splintering, the chains of command are snapping. If we hew to the old ways, we will be swept aside. Lord Layak has foreseen this – *I* have foreseen this.'

Jassim lowered his voice as they passed two black-robed serfs, who swept in the opposite direction, carrying a scroll of leathery parchment between them. Barnhart caught a glimpse of symbols scratched into its surface.

'It is not the first time that I have spoken with Lord Layak. He took an interest in me as a younger man, you know. He showed me things, shared truths with me. My strengths, my abilities... He saw my potential. Just as I see yours, lieutenant.'

Barnhart tore her eyes from the scroll before it was carried out of sight, and met Jassim's gaze. The commander had fixed his features with a sneering smile, his eyes hooded by thick eyebrows.

'There is space in the galaxy for bold men and women, Barnhart. I am bold. I will take what is mine. Follow my lead, and one day you too might rise to my level.'

The words rang hollow. She knew the ship better than Jassim realised, and she had realised minutes before that they were taking the most circuitous route to reach the Astartes' decks.

His smile flickered, and she saw it in the flesh.

Jassim was afraid.

The halls of the *Unwilling Sacrifice*'s Astartes' decks were much larger than the lower decks, but, if anything, were even more sparsely illuminated. Figures moved in the shadows at the peripheries of the chambers and corridors, shuffling shapes, details of their forms hidden by hooded robes. Eyes seemed to be watching the two soldiers from under those robes, their movements tracked by whispers that hung at the edge of audibility and comprehension. Barnhart shook off another shudder, feeling powerfully out of place in the lair of the Word Bearers.

The entrance to Layak's personal chamber was much the same as others on the deck. Simple slabs of stone framed a weathered metal door, the only ostentation a sharp, angular script that had been carved into the rock. The architecture reminded Barnhart of the temples that had once been raised by the Legion on compliant worlds, spartan and utilitarian.

Jassim stopped before the doors, his way barred by two serfs.

As with all the others they had seen on their journey, their faces were hidden by voluminous black robes.

'Commander Jassim Feghorand,' he said, using the same voice he used to address his troops. 'Stand aside. I have an audience with your master.'

'My lord is in study,' came a voice from under a hood. 'He cannot – must not – be disturbed.'

'Nonsense. He requested my presence.'

There was a hiss under the robe. A laugh.

'Listen here,' the commander said, venom in his tone, 'I will have you flayed if you don't–'

'Enter.'

The voice came from the air itself, and was so deep that it made Barnhart jump. The serfs drew aside, still hissing softly, and the door slid open. Barnhart and Jassim stepped inside.

As personal quarters, the chamber was expansive, with space for an armouring table, a cot large enough to support Layak's transhuman bulk, and a space for prayer, but it had been made to appear smaller than Barnhart's own quarters by the hoard of items that filled its confines. Tomes and scrolls, tablets and data-slates, open at pages or passages written in myriad scripts that she could not recognise, rested on every surface. Books were held open by idols of glass and stone, wood and hair, intricate carvings and slabs of graven imagery. An array of swords, knives and other painful-looking devices that may have been ceremonial weapons were hung from the walls. Many had been removed from their designated locations and were scattered across the floor, as if the occupant had been practising combat with them, before being distracted and casting them aside.

It must have been the plunder of a hundred worlds, Barnhart thought, so different was each item. Each one must have been chosen, retained for some purpose, but no consideration seemed to have been given to their arrangement or categorisation. If it had not been the chambers of a Space Marine – one of a rapidly rising rank, no less – she would have thought the room lived in by some kind of covetous rodent.

The owner of the items sat at a writing desk in the centre of the chamber, illuminated in a pool of golden light by a single candle. His head was covered in the red cowl of a robe, and was angled downwards, his attention absorbed in a tattered book. He wore most of his armour, even at rest, the bulky plate embellished with carvings and scarred with runes, only his left arm bared. Some of his brothers had taken to daubing their armour red, but his plate was still the stone grey of the Legion's past. It made him appear as if he was another artefact in the chamber – an ancient object, suffused with lost knowledge, brought here from its resting place.

Until he spoke.

'Welcome, Commander Jassim.'

Jassim stepped forward, dropping to a knee and placing an open palm over his heart. Barnhart followed suit, trying to copy the unfamiliar pose as best she could, and felt her own heart against her fingers, thumping hard and fast in her chest.

'Thank you, my lord. I and the Children of the Blessed Moon stand at your command. I have studied as you requested, and–'

'You have brought another.'

Jassim stammered, thrown off by the interruption.

'Y-yes, lord. Lieutenant Yergorin Barnhart. One of my promising officers.'

The red cowl lifted as the Space Marine raised his head to look upon her. Most of his features remained hidden, but for a moment she saw the bridge of a nose, lit by the candlelight. His skin was pale, even in the yellow glow.

And then it was gone again, retreating into darkness as his gaze shifted, fixing instead on a small globe on his desk, rendered in dark metal. He picked it up with his massive hands, and raised it into the candlelight.

'I dreamed of a world,' Layak said. Markings etched into the globe's surface caught the light as he turned it around in his hands. 'A world of mountains and rivers, of deserts and of ice. A world of life, and of death.'

He set the globe down.

'I have never set foot on this world, but I feel I *know* it, even from a dream. Do you find that strange? That one can know something to be so, without having seen it with one's own eyes?'

Jassim made a demurring sound, preparing to answer, but once more, Layak cut him off.

'I was addressing the lieutenant,' he said. His voice was soft, but it seemed to slip into her ears – as if he was speaking from behind Barnhart, even as he sat at his desk. She gulped, her mouth suddenly dry as paper.

'You describe faith, my lord,' she said.

The globe stilled in Layak's hands for a moment as he appeared to consider the answer. Under the cowl she imagined eyes taking her in as a predator sizes up its prey. With an almost imperceptible nod, he began rotating the metal sphere once more.

'I do, lieutenant. I am a man of faith, and so, I searched for this place of my dreams. I could find no such matching world in my Legion's annals at first,' Layak said. 'But I am also a seeker of truth, and I have access to knowledge that my brothers do not. I found the world in the depths of the void.'

Layak gestured, and a bound book slid across his desk, coming to rest under his bare palm. He opened the book, leafing through it with a surprisingly gentle touch, until he reached the relevant page, placing a finger against the parchment.

'It is called Helwain, and it was registered compliant to the Emperor's false regime by my own Legion one hundred and fifty years ago. Unremarkable amongst hundreds, this world, but when my brothers landed, we found a people yearning for truth, and we obliged them, building them cities and temples in the Emperor's name.'

Layak shook his head, disappointment manifest.

'We were naive, then. We cursed the people to worship of a lie, and then we left to continue our own doomed crusade, leaving only a garrison force on the planet. The garrison was ordered to report each year, providing materials to the crusade and the Legion, but communication ceased some twenty years ago. Against the backdrop of our holy war, Helwain's silence has not been noticed. Until now.'

He closed the book with a snap, and rose from his seat, stepping out from behind his desk. Pistons slid and tubes pumped fluid in his armour, but he made not a sound as he stepped before the kneeling soldiers, his movements as silent as Jassim's own padded footsteps.

The Space Marine stopped in front of Jassim, so close that the older man was unable to crane his neck to meet his hooded gaze. Barnhart found herself focusing on runes that had been scratched into the grey-coloured armour on Layak's knee, instead. He was simply too massive to take in otherwise.

'I will travel to this world,' Layak said. 'The Children of the Blessed Moon will accompany me. Together, we will bring this world back to the fold. Assemble your forces. We will leave on the frigate *The Path Less Travelled*.'

'Yes, my lord,' Jassim said, slapping his palm against his breast to signal his acknowledgement. 'I will liaise with the other elements of the compliance force and prepare the company for travel immediately.'

'Other elements?' Layak asked.

'Apologies, my lord,' Jassim said quickly. 'I presume we are travelling with a Legion force, then? I will leave such logistics to you, of course. It would be an honour to fight alongside more of your brothers in the Word Bearers.'

'No other forces will be joining us on this expedition, Jassim. Are your Children not fit for their purpose?'

'They are, my lord!' Jassim stammered, stumbling slightly as fatigue set into his legs. He righted himself, balancing again on one knee. 'But with all respect, one company and one Space Marine... This is not enough to conquer a world.'

A silence chilled the air of the chamber. When Layak broke it, his words were shards of ice.

'You doubt me, after all you have seen. All that I have given you.'

'No, lord! Of course not! You are mighty, and my Children stand ready to serve, but...'

'Speak your mind,' Layak said, as Jassim's nerve started to fail.

'But... what if this Helwain has been taken by Guilliman's Ultramarines?'

Barnhart saw Layak clench his fists at the mention of the XIII Legion, a gesture of anger that struck her as very human.

'Then you will meet them in battle.'

'But my lord... we will die!'

Fast as an electrical spark, Layak lifted Jassim from the deck by some unseen force until he was floating alongside Barnhart. Agony contorted his body, his eyes bulging and his boots kicking to reach the ground below like a man being hanged from a gibbet. Whispers reached Barnhart's ears that seemed to come from the walls themselves, insidious and insistent, breaking the laws of reality with their configuration of words.

Layak stood still before the hanging man. Two points of golden light burned in the darkness under the cowl, bright and unblinking.

'Then you will die,' Layak said, and the finality in his voice opened a pit in Barnhart's stomach. 'You will die, and as your breath leaves your body, you will thank the gods that your final act in this plane was to pave my path to glory with your bones.'

Layak traced Jassim's cheek with the index finger of his left hand. Tattoos traced down his bared wrist, oil-black against skin so pallid that it appeared to have been drained of blood. Jassim's mouth worked, expelling a croak of fear.

'I believed you had a part to play in what is to come,' Layak said. His fingernails were long and sharp, and they inked a line of red blood along Jassim's jaw. 'But I see now. It was not you. You lack faith.'

An audible crack split the chamber as the bones of Layak's hand started to stretch, the skin splitting as his fingers elongated to form fleshy tentacles. They palpated at Jassim's face, testing for openings until they came to the orifices of his mouth and nostrils, where they slid inside like worms searching for warmth. Jassim's eyes reddened as Layak's monstrous hand probed deeper into the depths of his skull, silent horror etched in their sclera, until the Space Marine stopped, seeming to find what he was looking for. At a whispered command, the tentacles reversed their unholy growth, retracting once more with wet bone crunches, pulling something with them from inside the man's head.

Jassim's brain met the air of the chamber quivering, stretched and abused by Layak's monstrously changed fingers, but still in one piece. Wet ropes of nerve and spinal tissue extruded from Jassim's nose; fibrous and fleshy, they tugged at the brain's base, threatening to tear the organ apart, before their tensile strength failed and they snapped, whipping back into the dying man's face like a recoiling snake.

Disconnected from its body, Jassim's brain floated in front of him – grey, shot through with the indigo blue of uncountable blood vessels below its surface and smeared with black-red fluid. Barnhart was unable to tear her eyes from the organ, and she followed it down as Layak let it fall to the ground. There was barely a sound as Layak crushed Jassim's brain with his armoured boot – the only reminder of the commander's life and memories a dark stain on the chamber floor that remained when Layak drew back his foot.

He turned to Barnhart.

'Stand, lieutenant,' Zardu Layak said.

Barnhart's chest ached, and she realised she had not taken a breath in minutes, paralysed by the terror of what she was seeing. She refilled her lungs and stood on legs that shook with both fear and fatigue.

'Yes, my lord,' she said.

'Do you have faith?' Layak asked.

The Children of the Blessed Moon had not always been named so. Barnhart had joined the regiment when it had been known as the 117th Koifaul Light Infantry. Like most of her friends, Barnhart had been inspired by the stories of the Emperor that the Word Bearers had brought to Koifaul. They had been zealous converts to the Imperial Creed – a welcome change to the monotonous agnosticism of their parents' generation – and happily signed up for military duty as soon as her city's barracks were reopened. She had seen her father weep for the first and last time on the day she had departed her home world, tears of worry streaking his round face. She had cried, too, but they were tears of fierce pride. Belief had filled the void in her heart.

The memory came to her now. It felt like a lifetime ago.

'Yes,' she lied. 'I have faith.'

'Good,' Layak said, and she thought she heard a smile in his voice. 'I saw more than Helwain in my dream. I saw others – three who would stand against me, and two who would join me on my path. I thought your commander was one of the chosen, but I was wrong. I saw *you*, lieutenant.' He lifted his bare hand to her cheek now, and she stiffened, terror catching her breath. She dared not move as the talon of his fingernail ran carefully against her skin, sharp, but not breaking the surface.

'Such an inconsequential being, and yet… the gods have made their choice.' Layak paused for a moment, silent in thought, as if receiving a vox-transmission, before speaking again.

'You will guide the Children of the Blessed Moon on Helwain, Lieutenant Barnhart.'

The finger was at her chin. With the slightest pressure, Layak tilted her face upwards, baring her throat.

How could she refuse?

'It will be my honour.'

Layak let his hand fall. 'Your greatest,' he said, before turning and striding back to his desk. He reached for the metal sphere, and took it in his unarmoured hand.

'They will not follow you, of course – not at first. They will ask what happened to the commander. But that does not matter. I was right, in part – he does serve my purpose.'

The eyes were glassy and dead, but Jassim's body remained suspended in the air, his legs no longer kicking with terror. Brainless, his limbs twitched only occasionally with spare electrical signals, his heart slowing without a mind to control it.

Layak stepped before him and raised the metal sphere in his open palm, cupping it close to his cowl as if he was soothing a young bird. Responding to his whispers, the sphere clicked open, splitting along invisible seams to reveal a darkness inside.

At the opening of its shell, the darkness stirred, viscous and thick, before rising like oily smoke from the sphere. Neither a gas nor a liquid, the smoke seemed more like an animal – some kind of serpent, flickering at the edge of reality, its sinuous movements seeming to taste the air. Layak brought the sphere closer to the hanging corpse, and the smoke snake began to shake with apparent excitement. As Layak had before, it palpated at Jassim's face, leaving smears of thick gloom against his dead skin, before it finally found space around his bloodshot left eye. It pushed its way under his eyelid, narrowing its body to squirm past the eyeball, slipping more of itself into Jassim's skull until even its black tail had disappeared from sight.

Jassim's corpse began to twitch. Intermittently at first, suspended limbs jerking as if prodded with a shock gun, but then with more and more regularity until the body was thrashing so hard that it threatened to tear itself apart – like a smaller animal caught in the jaws of some dread canine. Barnhart heard joints pop and bones crack, and she wished she could close her eyes, block her ears, to keep the sight and sound out.

And then it was over. Jassim's body slowed. Its limbs righted themselves, bones working back into joint with wet popping sounds. Layak whispered a word, and the body lowered from where it had been suspended. It descended slowly, carefully, until Jassim's combat boots touched down on the deck below. Barnhart expected it to crumple to the ground, but ice prickled in her spine as it stood instead, coming to rest upright on steady legs.

Barnhart had seen many things in her long service, but she could not help but gasp as the corpse turned its head to face her. Its mouth was slack, its nose black with drying blood, but its eyes...

The corpse blinked.

'Barnhart,' Layak said, barely a whisper. The word stole the scream from her throat.

'Yes... yes, my lord?'

'Are you afraid?'

She stood on a knife edge. The wrong answer – she had seen what could happen.

She had to have faith.

'Yes, my lord.'

She heard a soft, wet sound. Under his cowl, the Space Marine licked his lips.

'What does it feel like?' he asked.

The strangeness of the question stripped her defences, just for a moment, and she spoke before she planned to.

'My lord?'

'They say that we cannot feel fear, my brothers and I. Did you know that?'

'I... had heard it said. A boon for a warrior.'

'We were made to fight for humanity,' he said. 'We feel anger, pain, sadness, and loss. But we do not feel fear. That emotion was taken from my kind. I wonder what they denied us.'

Barnhart's heart seemed to beat in time with the flickering candlelight of the room. Jassim's corpse regarded her still, its open mouth working wordlessly.

'I have become a student of emotion,' Layak continued. 'By interest and by necessity, I have learned what I could about the depths of emotion – the peaks of ecstasy, and the valleys of misery. Let me tell you a truth of this galaxy, Barnhart. Fear is all. This galaxy is shaped by fear – the fear of the unknown, the fear of failure, the fear of the truth.' He paused, and the light in his eyes flashed brighter than she had seen. 'And we are denied it. So I ask, your fear – what does it feel like?'

She started to answer, and stopped herself. How to describe a constant companion? Fear was as much a part of her as her lungs, her kidneys, her heart. It had joined her as a poison coldness in her gut as the transport rattled its way out of Koifaul's atmosphere for the first time. But it was a changeling. It became hot flashes behind her face as solid slug shots chased her across the stinking marshes of Panshaal; it was ice knives in her spine as she waited for the transport doors to open, letting in the green, curling smoke of the gassed city of Trencher's Maw. She felt it now, on a clanking ship in the blackness of the void, in a chamber of profane artefacts with a transhuman giant who had eyes of flame and a face of coiled darkness.

'It never leaves me,' she said. 'I know that I will only be free of it when I am dead. I have fought many battles, and I have seen the face of death more times than I would like to count. You are right, my lord – it is fear that defines us. It is fear that I have seen etched on the faces of men and women as their lifeblood drains away into the mud and dirt of some hell world. Only when they are gone does the fear leave them. They are almost peaceful then – their faces, I mean. I used to wonder why, and now I know. They have gone, and so has the fear.'

He was staring at her, head tilted to one side, as the words tumbled out of her.

'I envy them, my lord,' she said, and felt her face flush. 'To be without fear, finally. I think death is a door. There is a moment, at the very edge of life, where we must step through to the other side. But I am afraid of making that step. Do you understand, my lord?'

Twin pyres burned in the darkness of the cowl. Flames lit on the fuel of a trillion bodies. Enough to see the whole galaxy burn.

'I do,' Zardu Layak said.

Layak's rank as a captain of the Ashen Circle afforded him many privileges in his Legion, but even so, it had been strangely easy to commandeer a capital ship. At every turn, his brothers and superior officers were focused elsewhere, planning for the upcoming attack on Calth, or manoeuvring for their own advancement. They did not notice the transfer of a unit of soldiers to the vessel chosen – the frigate *The Path Less Travelled* – nor the crewing of the ship with Layak's acolytes. A lesser man may have called it suspicious, but Layak put it down, as always, to faith. It was meant to be.

He had taken the master quarters aboard *The Path Less Travelled*, but he spent most of his time in the ship's archives, its long armaglass window affording him a prime view of the world that he had only seen before in his dreams.

Even now, knowing what he had come to know, as he prepared for the descent to Helwain, he prioritised the mundanities of war. He disassembled and oiled his axe-rake, ensuring that the chain ran smooth through the wheels and motors of the ancient weapon, sharpening its teeth until they could cut skin at the slightest brush. He attended to his armour, ensuring not simply that the incantations etched into its surface were accurate to the texts, but also that the seals were tight and that the turbines in his jump pack were clear of obstructions.

Only when he was satisfied with the earthly preparation for making war did he turn his attention to prayer. Once, he would have offered his faith to the Emperor, but his new prayers beseeched more esoteric masters. They had been given form and description by Lorgar, by Erebus, by sages amongst his Legion, and by the scraps of truth found amongst his own collection of literature, and he had seen the truth of their power.

He had asked them for protection, and they had granted it. His body had grown with his armour, plasteel cables joining with flesh, ceramite swelling and heaving as it bonded with skin beneath. He had asked them for fortune, and they had granted it. Sergeants and commanders in his path died mysteriously, leaving the way open for command of his own Ashen Circle, his own expedition. He had asked them for guidance, and they had put him on this path. The path that ended with the light that he had seen – the all-encompassing brightness, the rapture. The path to glory.

He asked now for courage.

'Grant me the strength to do what must be done,' he said.

'We cannot do that,' Lorgar responded. His father stood in the corner of the chamber, his massive form at once there and not there, like an afterimage on an augury scanner after a nuclear blast.

'Father…'

'You have come so far, child,' Lorgar said, and Layak felt a bright star of pride burst in the blackness of his being. 'We have shown you the truth of this cosmos, and we have blessed you with our boons. Your devotion has been noted, but…' The Lorgar figure seemed to pulse with sadness. 'There is still weakness at your core.'

The darkness of the chamber started to split open, like static on a cogitator screen, until – grain by grain – it was replaced by a grey wasteland.

Monarchia.

The towers that rose into the sky were cracked and broken teeth in the skull of the city, profane monuments to a dead god who rejected their glory. The sky, once a perfect blue, writhed with storm clouds, thunder calling out its roars of anguish. Its people, once pious and devoted, were flakes of black ash, greasy, burnt motes of humanity left to drift in the wind.

A future denied. A dream destroyed. A heart broken.

'I will atone for this atrocity,' Layak said.

'Oh, child,' Lorgar said. 'This is not the source of your weakness. It is merely a step along your path.'

The wind picked up, and the ash of Monarchia was carried away with it. Layak was standing on a deck of stained metal. Glow-globes bathed him in red light, the colour of blood. There were screams on the recycled air.

His hands were small – much smaller than they would become – and they were full. He clutched fetishes and bracelets, charms and trinkets. Books, too, hugged to his chest. He kept them close, because they were all he had ever had.

'A meaningless life,' Lorgar said. He spoke in the boy's head. *'But you gave it meaning. A scaffold upon which to build something greater. Something worthy. Belief.'*

He turned to find Lorgar in this place, but the red room

was empty. Even the screams were dying. They were joined by a pounding – a rhythmic tattoo that shook the deck, and his young body with it. He looked up as the pounding increased in volume, and saw a monster, so tall that he had to crane his neck to take it in. A giant washed in crimson, with crimson eyes and crimson dripping from its sword. It stared at him.

He should have screamed. He should have run.

He stared back.

He woke.

The frigate *The Path Less Travelled* was much smaller than the troop transports that Barnhart was used to travelling aboard. Its corridors were sparse and narrow, squeezed in close to the spine of the ship by its builders to afford more space to weapons batteries and countermeasure arrays that specialised the ship for void combat against smaller fighter-scale craft. It had only one deck with crew quarters, and Lord Layak had taken it for himself, deeming it off limits for all but those he summoned. That left the five hundred soldiers of the Children of the Blessed Moon to find berths amongst the ammunition storage and engine decks. With no mess halls or briefing chambers available, they met instead in the frigate's hangar, the only space large enough to house them all at once.

Jassim stood atop a walkway in the hangar's upper reaches, preparing to address his unit. He appeared much as he had in life – tall, broad-shouldered, his leathery face folded and lined like a well-worn satchel, what remained of his white hair scraped backwards along his scalp. His uniform was immaculate, the grey jumpsuit tight to his body, the red robe over his shoulders wrapped intricately and secured with a brass brooch that denoted his rank. Older than most that served him, but still he appeared vital, ready to lead his troops into another battle on a new world.

Only Barnhart knew the truth. The commander was dead, a walking corpse that did not breathe, animated by something she could not explain.

The corpse-Jassim spoke.

'Children of the Blessed Moon! Today we join our masters once more in war. Of the entire fleet, we have been chosen for this task, and we will repay the faith of the Legion tenfold. Turn your faces to our fate, Children.'

The unit turned as one, angling their heads towards the grey-green world that hung suspended in the void, visible from the hangar.

'Behold. Helwain. Our masters once claimed this planet, but it has rejected their glory. Now it stands silent, awaiting our arrival to bring it back to compliance – to bring it back into the light. The world's primary hive has been abandoned by its population, and augury scans show that there is a new settlement in the forest that lines the world's equator. That city is our target.'

The commander raised a fist, a gesture of strength.

'We will join our masters, and bring Helwain back to compliance. To your landers, men and women of Koifaul! May the Blessed Moon guide us this day!'

The roar that filled the deck was sustained. The thing on the walkway spoke not just with Jassim's voice, but with his oratorial skill as well, controlling his audience with the practised ease of a preacher familiar with their flock. Ceremony was important to the Word Bearers, Barnhart knew well from two decades amongst their company, and it was just as important to the Children of the Blessed Moon as well.

The cheers finally died, and as soldiers began to filter towards the wide-bellied landers, guided by sergeants and officers, Jassim stood on the walkway, too still. A shadow darkened the doorway behind him, and Barnhart watched as Zardu Layak began to descend the stairs to the hangar deck.

CHAPTER TWO

The ghost haunted the city.

The world had been known as Helwain, but the city had no name in official records, built as it was after the planet's communications with the outside galaxy ceased some twenty years before.

The ghost knew it only as the city, but he knew its shape well. He moved in almost total darkness, through tunnels and halls of rough-hewn bedrock, deep beneath a massive stone ziggurat. He passed many others on his travels. Some of them joined the ghost for a time, walking in the same direction, until an unspoken command compelled them to branch off, following a different path in the warren of tunnels. None of them saw him, though. They simply moved past him as if he was not there, serene expressions on their faces.

He was not truly a ghost, not in the way such things have been understood throughout the millennia of human history. He had flesh, and bone, and blood. He breathed, and – technically – he lived.

He had not always been a ghost. He remembered a life in which he had been seen, had been touched.

He had been hated.

He had just been a strip of a thing, then. Just a child, in need of love and nurture as all children are. But his own family had shuddered and scrunched their faces as they gazed upon his features, and had rejected him. They sent him out into the world, alone. People had been crueller still out there. They had mocked him and kicked him, screamed at him and spat at him, all for the crime of existence.

Heartbroken, he had gone away. He hoped to find the companionship he had never felt before among the unnumbered ranks of soldiers in the Emperor's grand army, among the so many billions who had left their homes and travelled the stars together, bound by circumstance, honour, and loyalty. But even that had not been enough – he could not escape his very nature – and his new brothers and sisters had beaten and bullied the ghost, blaming him for shipboard accidents and deployment mishaps, cursing him as an aberration.

So the ghost had learned to hide instead. He found that he was good at hiding – very good indeed. He learned to harness the strange power – the same power that made him so hated – and shrank himself in the minds of others, using their revulsion to make himself almost completely invisible. With this power, he found he could walk amongst crowds as if he was not there, scarcely an echo of the man he had been.

And so he had come to this world pressed shoulder to shoulder with those brothers and sisters, amongst them already as a ghost. Their unit had been known as the Blood Gospellers, and they had been ordered to garrison the planet Helwain. They would replace an existing garrison force – a unit known as the Guld 27th, from a world the ghost had never heard of.

The ghost still clung to this memory, as bitter as it was, of a time before this world. The simple statement of purpose, imparted by the unit's commanders to all their troops, became his mantra – words he would whisper to remind himself that he was still alive.

'I am Private Dasich Shaav of the Blood Gospellers. Attached to the Word Bearers task force Echo of Khur, sent to relieve the Guld Twenty-Seventh from compliance duties.'

Shaav had studied the Guld 27th while en route to the world, as his brothers and sisters built their bonds of companionship. They had been a proud unit, decorated by the Word Bearers for their piety and devotion. They marched under a banner of stars – a constellation visible from their home world that their legends said depicted the coming of Lorgar. Their commanders carried sand from that world in vials, and only opened those vials when battles were won, scattering the grains to show that all worlds were one in the eyes of the Emperor.

But Shaav had not found the Guld 27th when he arrived on this world. He had found nothing, at first. The Blood Gospellers had landed in the planet's biggest hive city, its designated capital – a location close to water sources, with functioning power stations and mass-transit systems. It was empty. Shunt-cars ran in an endless loop between silent factorums and deserted hab-blocks, opening their doors on cue for no one, in a city of nothing.

It took them a week of high-altitude scouting, but the Blood Gospellers finally found their quarry. What they had become, anyway. They were in the forest. The city's people – its soldiers and civilians, its adults and children, its men and women – had willingly abandoned their civilised existence and returned to the dark forest that ran astride the equator of this world. There, they had clawed tunnel networks out of the soft rock that lay under the loamy soil and built a new city, in which they lived in colonies like insects.

Some collective compulsion had called the people of this world back to the primordial dirt and slime, and rather than guide them back to enlightenment, the Guld 27th had joined them.

Together, they had built. A great structure rose from the centre of the city, a tower of terrifying scale and maddening complexity. Stones of all shapes and sizes had been carved, carried, and placed by human hands, swelling the size of the ziggurat that rose into the white sky.

The Blood Gospellers had tried to land their drop-ships close to the ziggurat. The unit's pilots had taken standard approach vectors, maintaining vox contact, preparing their craft to disgorge their troops in the heart of the city.

But something had gone wrong with the pilots, and the drop-ships had fallen from the sky. Shaav was lucky. His drop-ship came down in the forest, the ship carving a furrow through trees and into orange soil during a semi-controlled descent. Their pilot had reacted faster than her peers, but they had still taken casualties. Of the fifty Blood Gospellers in the hold, only twenty remained alive, the force of the impact killing the others outright. They had done what they could with meagre numbers, setting up a perimeter and salvaging weapons from the crash site. The drop-ship was beyond repair, and they could not raise a response from any remnant of the Guld 27th, nor the local populace. Eventually, after much discussion, it was agreed that a scouting party of five would make their way into the city, voxing their findings to the rest of the unit outside to determine how to proceed.

Vox-transmissions from the scouting party ceased as soon as they cleared the city walls. That was when the decision was made for the remaining survivors to enter the city together. With the Emperor's name on their lips and fear in their hearts, they made for the black gates. They had forgotten Shaav, but he had joined them anyway – even as an outsider, he did not want to be alone in the silent forest.

They had expected resistance, but the gates stood ajar and unmanned. They made their way through, moving towards the ziggurat at the centre of the city. Whatever had happened here, somehow they knew that they would find answers there.

They found the scouting party soon enough, or what remained of them. Their bodies had been pulled apart, arms and legs torn from torsos and left bleeding into the orange mud, jawbones ripped from skulls, locking their corpses in eternal screams. As they investigated, people appeared from the crude buildings, clad in rags, or wearing next to nothing at all.

The de facto leader of the remaining Blood Gospellers – she had been a sergeant, and was highest ranking amongst the survivors – barked orders, warning the people back, but they kept coming, eyes blank, clutching crude weapons in loose grips. One man came too close, and the sergeant struck him with the butt of her lasrifle. The hit caved in the man's cheekbone, fountaining blood from his ruined eye as he spun to the ground, but he barely seemed to notice the injury, climbing back to his feet and renewing his inexorable assault.

The sergeant called the Blood Gospellers to open fire then, but it was already too late. For every shambling person put down with las bolt or bayonet, three more seemed to take their place. The ghost even saw remnants of the Guld 27th's unit markings amongst the populace: scraps of red-and-gold cloth flashing under thick layers of grime, unit tattoos on filthy skin. They joined the mass, swarming what remained of the Blood Gospellers until they reached them, until they pulled their limbs and their heads from their bodies, compelled to murder by something in the depths of the city.

Shaav had run, fearing that he would be next to be pulled apart by smiling killers, to die and become a true ghost haunting this place of foetid gloom. But their eyes never fell upon him, his form as invisible to the people of this cursed place as it had been to those in his unit. He found a bolthole in the city – a quiet place between and behind makeshift hovels, sheltered from the frequent rainstorms – and did what he always did. He hid.

A decade passed as he watched the strange people of this world. They toiled day and night, working in silence, building the massive ziggurat at the centre of the city like drones constructing a vast hive. Over time, the ghost grew braver, venturing further into the city to find food, to collect supplies and parts. He dreamed of leaving the quiet city, of repairing one of the crashed drop-ships, and making it away from this place of horror, of finally finding his home amongst the stars, amongst people who would see and understand him.

Just dreams. He could not leave the city. He was bound here, cursed to walk its streets and tunnels by the need to eat, to sleep, to live, even if he could not call it a life.

He followed the people of the city on their routines. As they descended into the ziggurat, the ghost would track them through tunnels that led down into the depths of the structure, lonely and curious. Ever further, deeper, he would descend, braving the tunnels until fear took over, and he made his way back to the surface, following the tracks he left for himself.

Until one day, he found what lay at the base of the ziggurat.

The tunnels at the bottom of the structure were thick with flesh, clogged like arteries with a throng of humanity that the ghost had to pick his way through to pass. He crawled between stick-thin legs, and pulled swaying men and women aside to open a path. Even physical touch did not elicit a reaction from the citizens of this unholy city.

He reached a wide chamber, and sweat prickled the ghost's skin. Heat hit him like a wall, the combined hundreds – thousands – of bodies that had been drawn to this place. The ghost saw a carpet of writhing humanity, and at its centre, rising above the mass, a giant seated on a throne of twisted metal.

A blade rested between his legs, the giant's hand resting on the pommel, the tip pointed into the ground at the base of the throne. A great bloodshot eye opened in the heart of the blade. It swept across the chamber, surveying all it could see, and Shaav squinted his eyes shut as it came to rest on him. He felt the eye quiver in his mind, searching for the echo of a man that had been there, until suddenly, it swivelled, angling upwards and widening.

The mass of humanity moved as one animal, animated by a command from a single voice. He could hear it in his mind, this voice, an echo that bounced from the walls of his skull.

+Outsiders have come. Kill them. Protect me.+

Dasich Shaav retraced his steps, making his way back to the surface as a ghost.

Five troop landers fell to Helwain's surface, their black frames burning red as they descended through the outer layers of the planet's atmosphere. Each lander contained one hundred Children of the Blessed Moon, except for Yergorin Barnhart's. She travelled with seventy of her soldiers – three squads under her command – and Zardu Layak.

Barnhart had been invited into the front compartment of the lander, alongside the Space Marine. A small coterie of her most reliable soldiers had joined them: Adalwin, cradling his boxy comms array in his arms; Vilka, her head making bird-like movements atop her long neck; Palgen, her crash webbing loose, leaning against her long lasrifle like a crutch; and Ditmar, his eyes closed, head back against the lander's metal walls, trying to stop the contents of his stomach rising during the turbulent descent.

Ditmar was the biggest of them – the biggest of the whole unit – his broad shoulders bunched with muscle, but even he was dwarfed by the Space Marine who stood amongst them. Layak was more than incongruous amongst the Children of the Blessed Moon; he was impossible. He wore the shape of a human, with the same configuration of limbs as Barnhart herself, but she found him almost too massive for her brain to comprehend – as though his being expanded beyond his physical confines, filling the space around himself with his presence, with his history.

His grey armour plate was older than she was. It was ornately carved, symbols scored into the ceramite and inlaid with silvered and gilded trinkets: bones, skulls, and – most common – the brazen flame of his order, the Ashen Circle. The Ashen Circle utilised jump packs, Barnhart knew from her service with the Word Bearers, but Layak did not wear his for the expedition. Perhaps, she thought, because the twin turbine device simply would not fit inside a lander primarily designed to deliver human troops.

Layak's head hung low, as if deep in meditation. His cowl was gone, but still she could not see his face. In the robe's place he wore a helm of grey and bronze, the weathered metal framing a V-shaped eye slit that gave him a wrathful mien. Anger and hatred, locked on a face of stone. The eye slit glowed with the same dull red that burned against the lander's ablative armour, and Barnhart found herself remembering the twin points of gold light that had shone from the cowl. Eyes that watched her from behind the visor now, as Layak's head rose from his reverie.

She averted her gaze as the lander broke into the lower atmosphere. For a few moments, the air was calm, and Ditmar released a breath he had been holding, before the lander hit the cloud layer. They were thick enough that they whited out the world through the viewports, and shook the craft so hard that Barnhart had to swallow the bile rising in her own throat. She closed her eyes, then opened them again when two bright stars of gold opened in the darkness behind her eyelids. She found a rivet on the viewport to stare at instead, and willed the pilot through the turbulence and down to the ground below.

The lander punched through the base of the cloud, white wisps trailing behind its plasma engines. A smear of orange and green had been painted beneath its dark hull, the colours coalescing, taking shape as the grasping trees of a temperate forest as they descended closer. The landers formed up as they dropped from the clouds, coming in for a steep approach, Barnhart's craft at the rear. The trees covered the land like carpet, seemingly unbroken from horizon to horizon, until Barnhart saw their target: a wide-based tower of yellow stone, rising from a scar in the forest.

Augur scans had shown the city from above, but as the eight-sided ziggurat at its centre grew closer, the scale of the thing took Barnhart's breath. It rose far higher than any tree in the surrounding forest, casting a shadow across the landscape. Even kilometres away, Barnhart could see that it was almost organic in its construction, like the colony of some vast species of insects.

'Two kilometres out from target,' the lead lander pilot called over the vox. Jassim's voice followed.

'Prepare yourselves for disembarkation, my Children. Landers will set down at the base of the structure, and we will secure defensive positions before moving in to capture the target and pacify any resistance.'

'One kilometre from target,' the lead pilot called again.

'May the Blessed Moon smile upon you, my Children,' Jassim said. *'And may a new sun–'*

The vox-transmission died with a whine. Jassim's lander banked sharply, angling its nose towards the forest below, then dipping out of view. Flame erupted from the forest. The process took moments, faster than the landers behind could react, and the vox-channel filled with noise, panic and confusion before individual feeds were cut off in turn, and, one by one, the formation of landers dashed themselves against the forest below.

Barnhart unstrapped her crash webbing and threw herself forward, out of her seat, stumbling down the corridor into the cockpit of her lander. The hatch to the cockpit was closed, the hydraulic seals reading as *LOCKED*, but she tried the door anyway, shouting over open vox-channels as she wrenched against the handles.

'Children of the Blessed Moon, report! What's happening?'

Screams were her only answer, as her world spun. For a moment, she was weightless as the lander pitched sharply to the side, following its siblings towards the ground, turning what had just been the wall into the craft's new floor. Dragging herself to her knees, Barnhart heard thudding footsteps from behind, and only just managed to duck out of the way as Zardu Layak threw himself, shoulder-first, into the locked door. The metal frame buckled as the Space Marine's bulk collided with it, shearing the door from its hinges, and exposing the cockpit beyond.

The co-pilot turned at the almighty noise, while, somehow, the pilot's focus remained forward, hands on the craft's throttle and control stick. The co-pilot's eyes were glassy, his jaw slackened, and as Barnhart followed Layak through the door, the man turned back to the control console with a new focus, his hands sliding with expert grace across a bank of dials and switches, cycling engines back and shutting down critical flight systems.

'What are you doing?' Barnhart screamed, but the man had no chance to respond. Layak grabbed the skulls of both pilot and co-pilot, and wrenched them back from the control console with such force that they both tore free of their bodies.

Layak let the decapitated heads fall to the ground, and turned to Barnhart.

'Fly,' he ordered, his red visor flashing.

She'd only had rudimentary flight training during her service, but to argue would have been pointless. She unfastened the pilot's crash webbing, before booting his headless corpse from the command chair, its neck stump still pumping blood across vital flight apparatus.

'Hold on to something!' she called to her squad over the vox, as she pulled the flight stick right, trying to correct the steep dive.

The lander coughed apologetically, and tipped further to the left. Barnhart scanned the control panel, looking for the most important systems to bring back online. With time against her, she decided instead to start flipping the closest ones, hoping that one would reignite the engines.

She was only vaguely aware that the air in the cockpit was growing colder by the second, as Layak muttered words not designed to be spoken by human tongues. Things were moving too fast. She tried to breathe, to slow things down, to give her time to save herself.

Deep breath in.

She pulled back on the control stick as hard as she could, trying to pitch the lander's nose up.

Deep breath out.

A siren wailed in the cockpit – ground proximity alert. 'Pull up, pull up,' the cogitator blared.

Deep breath in.

She had always wondered how she would die. At least it would be quick. She closed her eyes.

Deep breath out.

In the blackness, two eyes opened. Then two more, and two more. Six golden eyes watched her from the dark.

Retro thrusters roared, and she snapped her eyes open. Trees crowded the viewport like an audience, craning their necks to look into the cockpit. The lander tore through them, their branches helping to slow its descent. Other forces, like unseen hands, seemed to take control of the lander, working with the retros to cushion its terminal fall, guiding it down to the earth below. Ice crystals formed at the edges of the armaglass viewport, and Barnhart shivered, suddenly aware of the unearthly cold.

Still, landing was a violent affair. The cockpit bore the initial impact, the lander driving into the orange mud nose-first, before the front of the craft bounced upwards, and it skidded on its belly for fifty, one hundred, two hundred metres until it came to rest against a particularly wide tree.

'We're down,' Barnhart said over the lander's internal vox, as much to herself as her troops. Pressing an illuminated button on the control console to open the bay doors, she stood from the pilot's seat on unsteady feet. Layak had already gone, and the ice crystals against the viewport were melting, condensing into water that ran like tears. She made her way into the crew compartments as running lights winked off, their red glow replaced by the milky white of the onrushing daylight. She shook off the afterimage of the six-eyed figure, allowed her training to take over.

'Disembark!' she called to her squads.

The landers were black blemishes against the pure white sky. Shaav thought they were birds at first, even though he had not seen birds in the two decades he had spent in the city. Only as they grew in size, and as he heard the feline growl of plasma engines, did he realise what they represented.

Salvation. Hope soared in his chest. Someone was coming – someone with weapons, with ships, with soldiers – to destroy this city, and take him away. A new life, somewhere else, another chance.

Hope died as fast as it rose, speared in flight as he realised what was about to happen. They were coming in too fast, too close. They were trying to land in the city.

'No...' Shaav whispered, as he started to make out details on the landers' bulky frames: cockpit viewports, glinting with reflected light; wide rapid-exit hatches for mass deployment. His whisper rose to an involuntary shout – 'No, no, no!' – and he winced as his words echoed from the stone walls of the city. They were harsh, like an animal's bark, and he shrank from them, instinct making him afraid that he would be heard.

The landers reached the edge of the city, and began their awful suicide dives towards the ground. The first clipped the city's outer wall on its descent, tumbling madly before slamming into the orange dirt and exploding with an earth-shaking boom. The second followed it in, plummeting hard and fast to the ground, as did the third, but the fourth seemed to stall, engines coughing as its pilot attempted to power them off mid-flight. It hung for a moment, its shape not suited for travel through the air but managing to glide on sheer momentum alone, before that momentum carried it into the side of the ziggurat. Shaav threw up his arms to protect his head as shards of broken stone peppered his body.

The fifth lander seemed destined to follow, but as Shaav watched, it began to buck against its fate. Plasma engines sputtered, alternating whines and roars, as the pilot pulled against the dive it had been sent into. The craft wobbled and rolled before stabilising, banking into a shallow descent that took it away from the city and out into the forest. Shaav waited for an explosion, for a fireball, but none came.

Hope rose again in his body, like bile in his throat.

He ran, towards where he had seen the lander come down in the forest, and towards his salvation.

* * *

Already, Barnhart's boots were coated with the rust-coloured mud that made up the forest floor, sticky and smelling faintly of copper. Thousands of sickly trees rose from that mud, their large leaves hanging lank from their crowns like greasy hair. The lander had carved a furrow through several of them, through which she could see the city beyond, and the ziggurat that rose from its centre.

The peak of the eight-sided structure rose far above the trees, stretching into the low clouds in the pale sky. The ziggurat *was* the city, in truth, its irregular sides stretching to the edge of city walls built from yellow sandstone. It was clearly not finished – crude construction equipment and human workers could be seen on its faces, manoeuvring vast slabs of stone into place. From a distance, Barnhart could see that they formed a series of interlocking shapes, zigzags and spirals that seemed there more to satisfy aesthetic principles than engineering concepts of reinforcement or redundancy. She wondered how it stayed up, and yet, somehow, it rose higher than the tallest towers of ferrocrete and plasteel that she had seen.

The walls below separated the city from the forest, carved of the same yellow stone, broken only by a large double gate of black metal, its face daubed with icons she did not recognise.

Seventy Children of the Blessed Moon made their way from the lander, some patching minor injuries, others simply shaken by the violence of the landing. Barnhart saw confusion and fear in their eyes, and knew that, without direction, it would soon become despair. She knew despair well.

Layak knelt in the dirt. At first, she thought that he too may have been dazed by their ordeal, but as she drew closer to the huge warrior, she realised he was carving something into the earth with his ungloved hand, long fingernails raking lines through the mud.

'My lord,' she dared interrupt. His finger stopped mid-stroke. 'Apologies, my lord, but… what are your orders?'

'Hold this position,' he said, his voice distant.

'Yes, my lord. I will inform the…'

Layak's head turned, his eye-lens flashing red.

'Hold this position at any cost, lieutenant.'

She remembered Jassim, and the way his dead eyes had looked at her. If they were to die here, then she would be sure they died fighting.

She raised her voice, catching the attention of the three squads in the clearing.

'I want Dimidiata and Cornicularis squads watching the treeline – set up fire positions from cover points close to our landing position. Novilunium Squad, begin a sweep of the immediate proximity. I want to know what we're dealing with here.'

They were slow to move. She fired her lasgun into the air, and the fizz of the bolt pulled their attention, faces turning to the sound.

'Children of the Blessed Moon! In Commander Jassim's absence, I am ranking officer. We still have a mission here. Form up in squads, and move!'

Barnhart turned as her soldiers broke into groups, checking weapons and pulling destroyed trees together to make makeshift barricades, and located her comms specialist.

'Adalwin, patch me into an officer-level vox-channel.'

'Yes, ma'am,' he responded, setting his comms array down in the mud and adjusting dials on its face. He nodded, and Barnhart spoke.

'This is Lieutenant Yergorin Barnhart, calling for any remaining Children of the Blessed Moon to make contact. Lander Five made a successful emergency touchdown in the forest, three full squads at my disposal.'

She scanned her eyes across the clearing. Layak stood now at the edge of the forest, watching the treeline like a hunting animal tracking a scent.

'Lord Layak is with me. We have his command.'

* * *

Shaav ran. Behind him, the city began to move as one, its mind-slaved population climbing from caves and tunnels, from huts and hovels, coming like white blood cells to kill or claim the outsiders in the name of their lord. His heart thumped in his chest as he ran, each beat the tick of a chrono. He did not have long to warn the newcomers before the city would be upon them.

He burst from the city walls and out into the wilderness beyond. The lander had come down close by, and he found the gash carved into the forest soon enough. Soldiers, in uniforms different to his own, but still recognisable as Imperial military – black jumpsuits, wrapped with red robes, carrying lasguns of an unfamiliar pattern.

'Hey!' he shouted. His voice was still alien to his ears – it had been so long since it had been used. 'Over here!'

Some of the soldiers wore light helmets of grey plasteel. Their heads turned, scanning the forest. They looked straight through him.

Shaav had become so used to hiding that it had become second nature, a glamour that he wore without conscious thought. He had to concentrate to be seen, and as he did, he saw himself for the first time since he had come to Helwain.

He was rake thin, his bare chest showing through the ragged remnants of a combat suit. A long beard protruded over that chest, its hair as matted as that on his head, dark and thick with grime and filth. Lines of stress and strain were carved around eyes of a dull grey, framing a mouth that housed teeth that had blackened with a lack of care. He stank, washed only in the rains that fell during the hot seasons, over months he had long since given up on counting.

'Identify yourself!'

'Don't shoot!' he screamed, shame and fear strangling his voice. He threw his hands in the air, cowering as lasgun barrels converged in his direction. 'Please, don't shoot! They're coming! You need to get out of here – *we* need to get out of here!'

A las bolt burned the air over his shoulder. A warning shot. One soldier spoke, louder than the others.

'Who are you? Answer me!'

He breathed, and let his mantra form on his lips.

'I am Private Dasich Shaav of the Blood Gospellers, attached to the task force Echo of Khur, sent to relieve the Guld Twenty-Seventh from compliance duties!'

'Where is your unit?'

'They're all dead, or...'

'Or what?'

'Or worse.'

'What do you mean?'

'There's no time! There's something in the city! Something terrible. Please, we have to get out of here, we have to...'

Shaav saw the giant in the shadow of a tall tree, and his blood ran cold. Its armour was grey where the thing in the ziggurat's was red, but apart from that they were the same – the same monstrous frame, the same inhuman armour, the same symbol, borne on the left shoulder: an open book, its pages aflame. Space Marines. Word Bearers.

Death made manifest.

The giant turned to him, a single red eye in its grey faceplate.

Without thought, Shaav hid. He imagined himself as glass, as nothing, too inconsequential for notice. The illusion worked on the soldiers. They raised their weapons and barked orders for him to show himself, but the giant's gaze was unwavering. The eye, staring right at him. Shaav stayed very still, silently sending a prayer to his Emperor.

'There you are,' the giant said.

Unseen hands pulled at rough material that had been wrapped around Shaav's head. The blindfold fell away, and a redness filled his vision, viscous and liquid, deep enough to swim in its depths.

'Where am...?' Shaav started, before coughs racked his body. He spat, phlegm and blood, onto the floor below.

His head throbbed, the pressure behind his eyes threatening to push them from his skull. He was upside down. Limbs bound, and suspended on an armature in the darkened chamber. Something had been scrawled onto the skin of his chest. He tried to angle his head to read the words, but his brain throbbed harder when he tried to make sense of them, and he gave up, letting his head fall back.

He looked around the room instead. His eyes acclimatised, and he recognised the interior of a spacecraft. The lander, he guessed. And he was not alone. He saw a shape in the redness. The Word Bearer.

Dread tensed his muscles in their binds. The giant was watching him.

It spoke.

'What are you?' the giant asked.

'Please, where am I?'

Blinding agony whited out his vision, so much pain that he could not scream.

'I will ask again. What are you?'

Shaav was panting like a dog. He took a deep breath, and repeated his mantra. He wanted the pain to stop.

'I am Private Dasich Shaav of the Blood Gospellers...'

Pain, again, so sharp and hard that he thought he would leave his body. It felt like the end of the world, and when it stopped, he vomited, retching the meagre contents of his stomach onto the deck of the lander.

'That was not the question I asked, Private Dasich Shaav,' the shape said. 'I know who you are, but I want to know *what* you are.'

Shaav concentrated, tried to make himself invisible to the thing that was hurting him. He tried to let the pain slip through his fingers, to become nothing once again.

The shape laughed. It leant close, and through watery eyes, Shaav could make out details. Its left arm was free of armour from the elbow down, and he saw it was adorned with tattooed script. The eye-lens at the centre of the helmet's faceplate was translucent in the reddened gloom. It hid the Space Marine's features, but Shaav thought he saw eyes, like two points of starlight, shining from its depths.

'I can see you,' the Space Marine said. 'You are a practised psyker, but such tricks will not work on me. I see the truth in all things.'

He traced two fingers in the air. Shaav felt his skin prickle as they drew shapes in the redness, unable to tear his eyes away. The Space Marine turned his hand over suddenly, exposing the palm. Shaav heard a spattering sound, like the cooking of meat, and the flesh of the hand started to bubble. The air itself howled, as if its individual molecules were being tortured.

The words tumbled from Shaav like the vomit from his mouth.

'They sent me to garrison the planet, said it belonged to the Word Bearers, to… your kind. There was a warrior in command of the city, they said, but when I got there, the soldiers, the people… they'd changed. They'd lost their minds! They killed us, my unit, and the ones before… they joined them. They didn't eat, didn't sleep, just built, and prayed to the thing that lived in the tower. It… he… he can control them somehow, he has a weapon…'

The stench of week-old corpse and lasgun afterburn hit his nostrils as a worm born of viscous darkness crawled from the giant's palm. The Space Marine raised the shadow worm, bringing it alongside Shaav's ear. He was frantic, bucking against his restraints, desperation in his voice.

'That's all I know, please, please, you have to believe me!'

Shaav could hear sounds like vox-static as the worm coiled around itself, an otherworldly hissing and popping that set his teeth on edge.

'And how are you here? How did you avoid the same fate as your brothers and sisters?'

'I used my… powers. They couldn't see me when I hid – *he* couldn't see me. I've been into the centre of the ziggurat, I know where he is. I can tell you, you and your brothers. Anything you want, please, just take me away from here.'

The worm slid back into the Space Marine's palm. The stench of rot dissipated as fast as it had come, and Shaav tried to breathe again, only to have that breath catch in his throat as the giant slid a long, curved knife from underneath his robes. He turned it over slowly in his hand, and the black blade reflected the lander's running lights, glinting red.

'What is his name?' the Space Marine asked, as he contemplated the blade.

'Whose name?' Shaav asked, panic raising his voice in register.

'The Word Bearer.'

He was back in the chamber at the base of the ziggurat, sweat soaking his torn clothes. The red eye flickered as it moved over him, and as he stared into its black pupil, he heard a word. A word on the lips of the city's thousands of servants. A name.

'Hebek,' Shaav said. 'He is called Hebek.'

Utterance of the name brought a memory to Layak's mind. It was buried deep, under layers of psycho-indoctrination, beyond surgeries that changed his body and his mind. Such procedures were meant to wipe the memories of a life before ascending to join the Astartes, but some persisted, strong enough to cling to subconsciousness.

A boy, alone.

The giant stood before him. It had killed the monks from whom he stole his trinkets, and it would surely kill him too.

He could run. He knew every inch of the orbital, every corridor and every vent. He could hide and wait, let them pass and continue his existence, staying alive for another day. A week. A year.

A lifetime, alone, in a dead station, with only ghosts to pray with.

No. He had spent his young life running, spent it hiding. A filthy life, subsisting on scraps – of food, of comfort, of knowledge. Better to end it here, on the tip of a crimson blade, than to live as a ghost.

There was power in words, the books had told him. So he stood. He opened his books, and he read from their pages. He clutched his trinkets in his hands, squeezing them so tight that they drew blood, and he stared down the giant. His words filled the void between them, dancing in the air, describing places and times and concepts and realities that he could not begin to understand, in tongues that had not been spoken in centuries.

He heard them, frail and fragile, as they coagulated in the air. He waited for death as he spoke his belief in the face of his end, but it would not come. Instead, the giant laughed. He laughed loud – loud enough to drown out his chants, so loud that the boy had to cover his ears. He squeezed his eyes shut and fell to his knees, rocking back and forth, even as he mouthed the words he had memorised. When he opened them again, the giant had removed its mask. A face like his own stared back at the boy. Larger, harder, covered in scars, but unmistakably human in aspect.

'Faith makes us strong,' the giant said. 'You might have a place amongst us, boy.'

Layak had taken the dishevelled man into the lander for interrogation, leaving Barnhart and her squads to set up defensive perimeters around the craft.

Barnhart would have pitied the poor wretch such a fate, had the man's entire presence not been so wholly repugnant. It was not just his appearance. Everything about him had disgusted her, to the point that she had felt physical revulsion so strong she'd had to suppress a retch as Layak marched him past her on their way into the darkened interior of the lander.

Her mind wandered, imagining the exotic tortures taking place on the other side of the craft's armoured hull, when her comms specialist called out.

'Lieutenant,' Adalwin said. 'Movement in the treeline.'

Barnhart swung her lasgun up in the direction indicated, and spotted the target against the vegetation. A man, clad in the same ragged clothes Shaav had been wearing, was moving towards the first barricade line. She heard the brace and prime of lasguns as her soldiers levelled their weapons at the man.

'Hold!' she called, lowering her lasgun and stepping forward. She could see the man with her own eyes, could make out his face as he walked towards her. His smile was a rictus grin, fixed to his face. His eyes were bloodshot, straining in his head as if they would burst from his skull with the slightest pressure. He carried a laspistol at his side. Its barrel was ornately carved – an officer's weapon.

'More, lieutenant! They're coming from the city.'

'I said hold fire!' she called. Layak had taken an interest in the first man. She would not be responsible for killing the second, if the people of this world were ready to welcome them with open arms.

Barnhart raised a hand towards the man.

'I am Yergorin Barnhart of the Children of the Blessed Moon. We are here on behalf of the Word Bearers, acting for Warmaster Horus. Submit to compliance, and there need not be any bloodshed.'

The man's head cocked. For a moment, he stopped in his march, and a shadow passed across his face. Recollection, perhaps, or an understanding, bone-deep, of what was to come.

'Take his weapon,' she said, ordering two of her soldiers forward with a hand gesture. They moved as commanded, lasguns raised towards the man's chest, stalking forward through the orange mud until they reached him. The closest soldier lowered his weapon, reached forward, and pulled the pistol from the filthy man's hand. He offered no resistance. His grin never faltered, and his eyes never blinked.

The closer of the two soldiers turned back to Barnhart, confusion in his eyes.

'We accept your surrender in the name of the Children of the Blessed Moon, the Seventeenth Legion, and Warmaster Horus. Your compliance will be rewarded in the Warmaster's new regime.'

Still his smile did not falter, but suddenly the man juddered, as if shot through with electrical current. Through exposed and blackened teeth, he spoke. The words were rasps, wind forced through a dead throat. They sounded as if they came from the trees themselves.

'No... compliance...' he wheezed, and closed his bloodshot eyes.

The man exploded. Roiling green fire ripped from his stomach, incinerating the two soldiers standing alongside him. There was screaming, and the treeline was suddenly alive with figures – first one, then ten, then a hundred. Each one walked as if in the same trance as the first man, and carried weapons in loose grips. She saw lasrifles and autoguns, stubbers and plasma guns – the armament of an army regiment – and cruder implements as well. Knives, spades, sickles, and clubs, like a degenerate hive gang of a bygone age. They made a noise as they moved, this mass. They were chanting, their voices joining to repeat a single word:

'Heb-ek, Heb-ek, Heb-ek.'

'Open fire!' Barnhart called. 'Defensive positions! Don't let them get close!' She keyed her vox, calling to the warrior inside the lander. 'Lord Layak, we are under attack!'

The ritual was an old one. They all were. For all their frailty, humans were a curious and tenacious species, and as they expanded across first their home world and then the galaxy at large, they could not help but test the very edges of reality. They required no complex technology, such rituals powered instead by the base building blocks of life: pain and rage, misery and despair. The food of the gods, measures of each handily contained in the very soul of the human animal.

Even the tools that he had collected from fallen civilisations across the galaxy were little more than devices for channelling and focusing such energy. The tool used in this ritual was no different, though it was, Layak thought, as he turned the black-bladed knife over in his hand, rather a pretty thing. Its handle had been elongated, rising to a wicked spike, supporting a blade that he had sharpened himself, using his own tools to bring it to an edge as fine as his axe-rake's chain links.

'The gods have given me many things, that I may better serve them in this realm. Power beyond the understanding of even my brothers.' He extended three fingers, and drew a slash in the air. 'And now, they have given me you, Shaav.'

Shaav could not speak, could not move, his voice and control of his body taken by whatever sorcery the Space Marine had performed. The red light of the lander seemed to darken, as if the blackness of the void was creeping in from the heavens above, drowning it out.

'We have different destinies, but you are like me,' the Space Marine said. He tapped two fingers first to his armoured chest, then to Shaav's chest. 'We have been saved.'

Shaav's body would not obey commands. His arms were dead, and his head swung forward and back, like a marionette whose strings had been cut.

'We are vessels, Shaav, you and I, our destinies written, our bodies to be guided by greater powers. You were destined to come to this place, just as I was destined to find you. I am beginning to understand why.

'The thing in the ziggurat. He was – *is* – my brother. He knew that I would come for him, and he has prepared. He used the Anakatis to build a fortress, to build an army. Power beyond his earning, true, but power nonetheless. They would cut me down before I could get close enough to turn the blade against him. He knows me well, my brother.'

The Word Bearer traced a finger along Shaav's cheek.

'But he does not know *you*. He cannot see you – will not see you – until it is too late. Until his army is elsewhere, and I am at the heart of his fortress. You, Shaav, will guide me there.'

A tear swelled in the corner of Shaav's eye.

'Do not weep,' the Word Bearer said. 'Rejoice, for you have something that so many of your species lack – a purpose. You will play host to something greater than yourself. Something that will change the course of the galaxy.'

Shaav concentrated, forcing all his will to form words.

'Host... to... what...?' he managed. His voice was a wheeze in his throat.

'To me,' the Space Marine said.

'Who... are... you?'

'I have had many names,' the Word Bearer said. 'And I will have many more. In translation, I am the Eater of Wisdom.' He leant in close, his golden eyes burning. 'But you may call me Zardu Layak.'

He traced the black blade down the back of Shaav's scalp, applying just the slightest pressure. Skin parted, revealing the skull beneath, the bone pink-white and glistening. Shaav could only whimper in response, terror stealing the scream in his throat. The Space Marine ran the same blade along his own wrist, tattooed script swirling as blood ran from opened veins, viscous and dark.

He turned the knife over, placing its blade against the back of Shaav's skull. He offered a prayer to the gods for their gift, and pushed down with enough force to slide the blade through bone, down deep into the grey meat of the brain within.

Zardu Layak felt the pain in his own body, searing and vital, as their blood mixed. The darkness congealed, and he felt himself fall into a new reality. Layak blinked and saw the chamber through Shaav's eyes. They were weak, a simple optic nerve and limited brain function registering the layered colours of the deep void as simple darkness. He yearned for the complication of colour that he knew dwelled between the stars, and felt a pang of pity for the species, that they could not see the truth of their universe.

Layak stood, testing his new limbs. They too were weak, their wiry muscles wrapped around thin bones. He stretched, and those bones popped in their joints, a staccato rhythm that joined the beating of his single heart. Against the chorus, there was another sound, too. Shaav was still in this body with him, his consciousness not totally destroyed by the ritual of joining. He was screaming, Layak realised, and a smile played across their face.

Shaav awoke to darkness. Not the primal darkness of night, nor even the fathomless darkness of the void. This was darkness as sensation – a yawning, desperate misery.

He tried to block it out, to focus on other things. He felt the rough fabric of his jumpsuit on his skin, the coldness of a blade in his hand, the weight of exhaustion behind his eyes, but – with a growing horror – he realised he could not control them. He turned the blade in his hand without command, then stood up from his seat without willing it. His body was no longer his own. He shared it with the creature that had brought such misery.

Recognition hit him like a bolter shell. He knew who had taken his body, and in the same moment, he knew his mind. Images flashed through his consciousness, sights that his human brain could not rationalise. He saw a thousand burned worlds, and a million burned bodies. They were but a pyre for what he saw at the top: the charred corpse of Monarchia – the Perfect City – its libraries ash and its towers laid low. In the ruins he saw a golden-skinned figure, shining almost too bright to perceive, his face swirling as he spoke silent words. He saw a secret kept, even from his brothers, and a new library, built from the profane and the wrong. He saw rituals and ceremonies, heard whispered conversations with figures in the darkness. He saw things that would drive a man mad to look upon, and no matter how hard he tried, he could not look away.

He saw all this and more, but even the magnitude of such visions was dwarfed by what he felt.

Shame. Shame, more physical and vital than he thought possible. Shame like an absence in the fabric of reality, like a sucking black hole, pulling in light from the universe around it. The scale of it took Shaav's breath away. The void consumed everything in a desperate need to be filled, beyond any scope his mind could comprehend.

This was why they needed such huge frames, Shaav thought – to contain such depths of sensation, to lock them inside a cage of steel-hard bone and muscle. Shaav wanted to cry, to retch, to tear off his skin, to do something to cast this thing out of his body. But he could do no such thing. So he did all that he could do. He screamed.

He felt his mouth smile in response.

Layak slipped from the lander in silence. He had met many psykers in his long life, but Shaav's powers were unique – with a talent honed by decades of misery and loneliness, the man could step outside of reality. Not into the warp – Layak himself had learned how to breach the fine boundary into the immaterium early in his forbidden studies – but outside of comprehension itself. So repugnant was he to other beings on this plane of existence that they simply would not take him in.

Wearing Shaav's skin, the Space Marine slipped past the Children of the Blessed Moon as a ghost. Las bolts flew over his shoulder as he started towards the city, past their targets: mindless thralls that were leaking now from its black metal gate, towards the landing site in the forest. Their eyes were wide and unblinking, but even they could not see him as he picked through their thickening ranks, stealing over corpses with las-bolt holes bored in their ragged jumpsuits, slipping between the hundreds of emaciated bodies that were making their way from the depths of the ziggurat at the centre of the city, out to eliminate the intruders.

The city was mud and stone, like the lost cities of Colchis' first peoples. A place of dirt and decay, primitive, and yet Layak could not help but be impressed by the scale of the endeavour. As he picked through its streets on Shaav's skinny legs, the ziggurat at its centre began to block out the sky, its maddening geometry a tribute to the knowledge and ingenuity of its creator. He saw, even now, how much work had gone into its construction, how much work was still going into it. Humans dotted the walls of the vast structure, like worker insects devoted to their tasks while the soldier caste battled outside the hive, shoring up foundations, repairing broken walls, and adding further to its peak.

The result was a grand monument, but a monument without purpose. This tower had not been raised in honour of the gods. It had been raised in hubris, in honour of one man. Selfish. Unworthy. Unchosen.

Layak reached the bottom of the ziggurat. Dark tunnels stood open in its orange stone base, roughly carved, as if clawed out of the earth by bare human hands. From the tunnels came a steady procession of thralls, creatures who had lived their lives underground. Their skin was pallid and hung loose from their malnourished frames, the white light of the outside world so bright to their unblinking eyes that they brimmed with tears. Their bodies were weak, their bones visible under papery skin, so close to death that their breath tasted of the grave – and yet, they chanted with one voice, speaking one word, loud and clear.

'Hebek!'

Shaav's memories were simple things, and Layak scanned through them with ease. They guided Layak to stores of food, places of shelter, but he did not need those details. The tunnels led down into the centre of the ziggurat, snaking together and apart to create a maddening tangle of possible routes. Layak found the memory at the depths of Shaav's mind, where terror had encircled it. A giant in red, a vast chamber in the earth, an unblinking eye.

Shaav's body knew the way to the centre, and to the thing that dwelled within the ziggurat. Layak let it show him the way.

CHAPTER THREE

Darkness and stinging sweat threatened to steal Shaav's vision. The man's muscles were nearing the point of exhaustion, but still Layak drove him on, deeper into the ziggurat, even as the man begged for mercy.

Layak wondered how humans could live with such weakness.

'An imperfect species,' Lorgar said. Layak turned, looking for his primarch, but saw only sweating stone, glinting in the darkness of the tunnel. *'But their souls persist, even as their bodies are remade. Even in you, my child. You are still tainted by shame, by mercy.'*

The darkness shifted, and Layak was rising from the tunnel on a plume of black smoke. Another place, another time, another memory – after Monarchia, after Lorgar had appeared to him in his dreams, but before the betrayal at Isstvan V.

They landed together, a flight of four angels coming to rest on the sandstone lip of the great opening. Layak killed the jets of his jump pack with a blink. Shadows leapt in as the engine glow abated, the darkness of the hollow rejecting the light. Still, he could see, and he offered praises to his gods for their gifts.

The hollow was vast. It appeared as an animal burrow, its edges organic, scraped and clawed with bleeding fingers, but Layak knew it was no mere shelter – even if it did provide a dwelling for the hundreds of mortals that now turned to face the angels who had touched down in their domain.

No, it was more than home. It was a cathedral. He had seen a hundred different worlds, with a hundred different religions, and yet, humans always worshipped the same way. Together. The weakness of the individual absolved by the strength of the whole. What is one life on its own? Only great, if given in service of something greater. Strength through sacrifice.

These people understood sacrifice. They ran towards their doom at the hands of the angels.

'Go,' Saucan voxed as a hundred unwashed faces gazed upon the four warriors. 'Burn the rot from this place.'

The worshippers moved as one, as their cousins had on the loamy forest floor. Layak flipped his axe-rake in his hand, revving the weapon's chainblade as he braced for the attackers to arrive. Next to him, Hebek ignited his jump pack, belching black smoke as he launched over the heads of the throng, but Layak resisted the urge to follow. He wanted to be amongst them – to feel their strength, and to show them their weakness.

They arrived as a mass, filth rendering them too similar to tell individual targets apart. Layak swung low through the meat and gristle with a backhand strike, shattering kneecaps and severing legs at the thigh. Upended by the force of the blow, bodies and body parts sailed out into the milky sky, those still conscious of their state joining their erstwhile colleagues in their final descent to the ground far below. Rising from his kneeling stance, Layak flicked gore from his axe-rake and squeezed the trigger of his flamer. He felt a whuff of pressure as fire leapt from beneath his wrist. He steadied his hand and hosed liquid flame across the second rank, blackening skin and melting eyeballs. Worshippers gibbered as they withdrew from the flame – the first suggestion that these people had any shred of self-preservation left in their souls – and Layak took advantage, stepping forward into the space carved.

The gout of flame illuminated the cathedral now, and he could see its structure. A ridge ran along its centre, from deep in the shadows at its rear to the edge of the cliff, where a pulpit stood to allow the cult's leaders to preach their creed to their degenerate flock. Embedded into the stone was an emblem, carved not as the cathedral itself, with bleeding fingers, but shaped with some kind of instrument. Whorled shapes decorated the object, three circles combining in repetition.

Layak recognised the pattern. He had seen it in his dreams.

'Cut them down!' Saucan howled. Their leader was always first into the fight, first to prove his loyalty to his primarch. 'For Lorgar!' he screamed.

He had proven his loyalty to the Emperor, once, but that had been before Monarchia. The trauma of the event had split the Legion's history into epochs – the before, and the after. Unable to quiet his fervour, it instead found form in the wild swings of his axe-rake through flesh, in the streaming wash of fire from his flamer.

'Come,' Hebek said, over a private vox-channel. 'The sergeant has successfully occupied the bulk of their forces. Let us find what we came for.'

Hebek ignited his jump pack. Its engines roared, their heat charring the skin of those unlucky enough to have been pawing at his armour. Layak followed a moment later, burning retros to check his ascent into the air, lest he careen into the sandstone roof above. The older Space Marine touched down over the heads of the mass, at the entrance to a dark tunnel that led into the rock. Like the cathedral itself, it seemed to have been dug with human hands. Blood, old and dried, was scraped along its walls.

'We descend,' Hebek said. 'Follow me.'

The tunnel was wide but made for creatures shorter than Space Marines, and both Hebek and Layak had to duck to make their way down. The path split after a few hundred metres, and Hebek paused.

'You want to make sergeant, boy – what would you do?'

Layak swallowed his immediate answer. He didn't want his brother to taste his excitement.

'We split up,' he said, as flatly as he could.

'Very good. I'll take the left path.'

'No.' Layak almost shouted the word. He collected himself, tried to control his tone, and spoke again. 'No, I'll take the left.'

Hebek snorted. 'So be it. We burn this place in the primarch's name.'

'In his name,' Layak echoed, and Hebek was gone, the light of his flamer growing smaller into the darkness until Layak could see it no longer.

Layak found the chamber at the end of the path. The things that dwelt within it had been human once, but he had only deduced that by the shape of their internal organs. He saw those organs as he carved them open with his axe-rake, and kidneys, livers, hearts, and lungs decorated the floor when he had finished, pumping blood and other fluids onto the ground alongside a baffling assortment of limbs and appendages, teeth and tusks. The once-human creatures had gibbered in apparent delight as he carved them apart, their ululating cries searing shapes and colours into his mind. They were only fading now, as tentacles and fingers slowed their twitching on the stone floor, and Layak looked upon the objects that had led to the ruination of this world.

They were such tiny things. A bundle of torn parchment, its surface stained, its runes half nonsense. A human skull with too many eye sockets, its crown splintered as if the brain inside had detonated violently. And a small, polished stone, its jet-black surface chased with lines of blue.

Layak ignored the parchment and the skull, focusing instead on the stone. It seemed to blink as he approached it. He picked it up, feeling its weight in his hand.

'What are you doing, boy?' Hebek asked. Layak spun on the spot, his finger on the trigger of his hand flamer. The older Space Marine regarded him through the slit in his helmet visor. It was illuminated red and orange, as if the man inside had been set aflame.

Layak felt the stone throb in his hand. His finger caressed the flamer trigger, and he saw a future play out. The stone-grey armour washed in red, the colour of fire, the colour of blood. An accident, he would say. Another martyr. A brother, fallen in glorious service. Only he would know the truth. His brother, killed to protect his secret.

Behind Hebek, in the shadows at the corner of the chamber, he saw Lorgar. Layak had stood alongside his father. The room he was in now was too small to contain his frame, but there he was, just as he appeared in his dreams. He smiled, and spoke without moving his lips.

'You must take the step, my child.'

Hebek repeated himself. 'I said, what are you doing?'

Layak let his flamer fall to his side.

'Nothing,' he said. 'Nothing. I am… I am simply observing the blasphemies these people keep.'

Lorgar dissipated, and Layak was left alone with Hebek. The older Space Marine tilted his helmet slightly – a small, quizzical movement.

'We are here to burn these things, boy, not study them,' he said, after a moment. His voice held no judgement – a simple reminder, like a father's guidance.

The tunnel made its final twist, and Shaav reached the chamber at the centre of the ziggurat.

It was vast. It had been carved from the same stone as the rest of the structure, but each slab was more carefully hewn, decorated with hieroglyphs and pictograms, describing shapes that made Shaav's mind swim. From Layak, however, he sensed familiarity. The Space Marine was reading the shapes as easily as words on a cogitator screen, venerations to powers that Shaav could not hope to comprehend. Braziers of black metal burned at intervals throughout the space, casting their hellish light upwards in a fruitless attempt to illuminate the ceiling far above.

A hundred humans remained in the chamber – those who had not been sent to purge the intruders. They writhed in supplication around the twisted metal throne at its centre, hands clasped, weeping in ecstasy. They were clad in the rags of Imperial army units, the firelight revealing uniforms and unit patches that Shaav recognised: the Makotan Stoneshapers, the Guld 27th, and – Shaav realised with a gasp – the Blood Gospellers.

They carried the same chant on their lips as the other thralls, but where it had been a war cry before, now it was an expression of adoration.

'Hebek!'

The object of their worship sat upon the throne. He was large – much larger than the worshippers who surrounded him – and wore armour the colour of crusted blood. His pauldrons were black as the void, even in the glow of the chamber, and they bore not only the symbol of the Word Bearers, but also a second device, etched on the other shoulder: a drawn gate, rendered in ochre. Layak wore the same symbol on his armour.

Hebek wore no helmet, and his hair and beard had grown long, both equal parts black and grey. His eyes were dark and unfocused, as if he was lost in some reverie. Across his lap lay a huge blade, easily as long as a man from hilt to tip. Its primary blade seemed to be carved from the orange stone itself, polished and honed to a wicked curve. But that was not the only dangerous part of the weapon. Secondary blades rose from its crossguard, alongside jagged and pointed objects that resembled nothing so much as horns, spines, and teeth. It made the weapon seem alive – an assessment helped by the red orbs that opened and closed on its twitching surface, like leering eyes in burned skin.

A word came to Shaav's mind. It was not one he had heard before, and instinctively he knew he was seeing a glimpse of Layak's own knowledge.

Anakatis.

As he thought the word, the Space Marine in the throne turned to look in his direction. For the first time on this world, Shaav was perceived, as the helmetless warrior's eyes focused on him. A flicker of confusion passed across his face as he took in the sight: a man, as dishevelled as those around him, in the tattered uniform of another world. But where the others knelt and chanted in supplication, this one stood defiant.

The Space Marine raised a hand and pointed an accusing finger, but before he could speak, Shaav heard a cracking sound. His body wrenched, twisted, and suddenly he was being pulled in half, his skeleton being removed from the meat and skin that surrounded it. He tried to scream, but the pain was simply too great, and he could only open his mouth. Saliva fell from his lips, drops making wet circles on the dusty stone floor.

Forced to his knees, Shaav saw a shadow of himself against the chamber wall as something massive split his body open. His ribs burst from his chest like searching fingers. Muscles in his arms and legs tore, leaving them to hang uselessly from the wreck of his torso. His organs – liver, kidneys, stomach – were thrust upwards through a too-small throat to be vomited from his open mouth.

The last thing Dasich Shaav saw with his own eyes before they were forced from his skull was Zardu Layak crawling from his back, his body somehow still relaying images to his mind as it died a traumatic death.

The Space Marine sloughed off the smaller man like a crustacean shedding its carapace, the discarded remnants sliding to the stone floor in a pool of blood and fluids.

Layak stood in front of his brother, his grey armour washed crimson in Shaav's viscera.

'Hebek,' he said. 'I have come.'

'Boy,' Hebek said. He held Layak's gaze, disbelief flickering across his face, before his craggy features crumpled with emotion. 'I had questioned whether you would return.'

'Here I am.'

Hebek looked down at the blade, then back at Layak, and when he looked up, his eyes seemed to brim with tears.

'Tell me, what moniker do you go by now?'

'I am Zardu Layak.'

'Of course, of course. The meaning is apt. I remember them all, your names. Even the first name you wore before you joined the Legion. When I found you. Should I remind you?'

'That child is dead.'

'I see that,' Hebek said. 'You have risen far. But then, you were always destined for greatness, boy – even I could see it from the moment I laid eyes on you. Others saw it, too. Kulnar guided you, tried to advise you, when you would listen. Saucan, curse him, was afraid of you. Always expected a knife in his back, that one. Paranoia is our Legion's affliction, but' – Hebek barked a laugh – 'maybe we were right. Why are you here?'

'My path led me here. I had a vision of the Anakatis blades. They are important to the gods, to be used in the next stage of their grand plan. I have come to claim them.'

'What will they be used for?'

'I do not know. I do not question the demands of the gods.'

Hebek snorted another laugh. 'Your name may change, but your faith remains constant.' He ran his hand along the length of the blade across his lap. 'The gods are right, though. They are powerful weapons.'

Layak stepped closer to the throne, into the light of the braziers, each footfall slow, measured.

'I was angry when I left the Legion,' Hebek said. 'When I left you.' He gestured at the thralls, still writhing in their dirt-stained rags. 'But I found something wonderful here.' He lifted the blade, heavy in his hand, laying the flat of it against his red vambrace.

Layak could hear the Anakatis blade as he moved closer to the throne, a low hum that sounded almost like voices from another room.

Hebek continued. 'We arrived on this world as exiles, clouded in shame. The Anakatis heard our arrival. They were waiting for us, they sang for us, and we answered their call. They gave us power in return, and I used that power as we were meant to.' He raised his arms to the chamber's ceiling, looking around in wonder. 'Look, brother. Look at what I have built, what I have given these people. I gave them salvation, and they have built this for me. For *me*. A place apart from power struggles or conflicts between brothers, where we can forget the shame of Monarchia, forget the conflict of our fathers.'

'There is no escape, Hebek. The gods see us all, and it is our duty to worship them. Lorgar found the truth, and you hide from it.'

'Lorgar found what he wanted to find.'

'He brought Horus to our side. The Warmaster believes in our cause.'

'Our cause.' Hebek scoffed. 'Horus believes in nothing but himself. He, of everyone, understands the galaxy as I do.'

Hebek weighed the Anakatis blade in his hand, and Layak saw the eyes on its surface swivel and blink. The older Space Marine raised the blade above his head, and the thralls suddenly stood, turning to face Layak as one.

'Why would I worship gods, when I have become one?'

'You are no god,' Layak spat. 'You have simply compelled these pathetic creatures to lap at your boots.'

'Then I am just the same as your Pantheon. They grow fat on the mewling supplication of lowly souls, do they not? Godhood is relative. The only measure is power on the scale we choose to comprehend. To the worm, the scorpion is god. I have given these people a place away from the pointless conflict, away from the grinding misery, the endless destruction. I have given them a paradise, and all I ask is their worship. They give it freely.'

'Freely!' Layak laughed. 'They worship the blade, not you.'

'What does it matter, if I hold the blade?' Hebek asked, hefting the weapon onto his pauldron as he stood from his throne. It was clearly heavy even in a Space Marine's hands, its serrated edge set into a haft overgrown with bone and teeth.

'We are broken, boy, can't you see it? Our father taught us to worship, *made* us to worship. He dug a hole in our hearts because he had a hole in his own. It will never be filled. We are a Legion of followers.'

He reached the bottom of the steps to his throne, standing on the same level as Layak.

'But I will not follow. Not any more. I choose to break the cycle,' Hebek said, lowering the Anakatis blade in a two-handed grip. 'And if you stand against me, I will destroy you myself.'

Layak's hand worked, calling forth his weapons. Black smoke trailed from his fingertips, sliding into his open palm and coalescing into the shape of his axe-rake.

'That honour is reserved for the gods,' Layak said.

Hebek growled, a sound like a hunting wolf, and his thralls ran for Layak, their anger mirroring the older Space Marine's own. Behind them, Hebek willed his charges on.

The axe-rake still partially formed, Layak swung a punch into the first thrall to reach him, caving the front of the man's skull in. Shaking what remained of the man's face from his fist, he hefted the chain weapon, and drove it, point-first, through the ribcage of another. He felt bone shatter, and continued the motion, sending the broken body careening into his compatriots, knocking them sprawling. They were pathetic things, the thralls, pale and malnourished, their skin etched with scarification that seemed to have been performed by unskilled hands. He recognised some of the shapes: three circles, the flaming eye, and – most common – the eight-pointed star, carved inexpertly into infirm flesh.

Layak clawed a ball of stinking flame from the ether, and hurled it forward, the fire sticking like glue to skin and burning like a plasma reactor. Behind his mindless army, Hebek dragged the heavy Anakatis blade, sparks shooting from the stone floor. He did not wait until his thralls were out of the way. The first swing was overhand, designed to split Layak in half from skull to stomach, but succeeded only in bisecting one of his own. Layak sidestepped, rolled, and came up to the left of Hebek, the flesh of his bare arm roiling as he called forth creatures from beyond the veil.

His recitation was interrupted as the older Space Marine worked with his momentum, carrying the vertical slice into a horizontal slash, using a second hand to stabilise the blade. Layak leapt backwards, outside the radius of the strike. Hebek was older, and he had not seen battle in long years, but he was still lightning fast, and the edge of the weapon scored a groove in Layak's ornate armour, defacing a line of scripture that had been carved across his chestplate.

So close to the weapon, the hum from the Anakatis was now a cacophony, the words clearer, more insistent. They offered power, strength, temptations beyond measure, if only Layak would take the weapon as his own.

Think of what you could do, child.

The words were clear, the promise true. Power, at his grasp, if he would only take it. He could be not a piece in the game, but the player.

No longer empty. The worshipped, not the worshipper. Take the blade, and rule this world, away from the galaxy. A god of your own making.

Layak tried to ignore the voice, concentrating on the thin veil between realities. On the other side, a long-legged being begged to be drawn through, its fangs already wet in anticipation of the rich taste of blood, and the pain it would bring. If Layak could only find where to cut…

His focus was stolen. He saw a city, a place of temples and beauty, with him at its centre. A new future. A new Monarchia…

'No…' Layak said, trying to force the image from his mind. 'No! That is not my destiny.'

'There are no gods, and no destiny!' Hebek roared. 'There is only power, and power is free to be used by those who take it. We worship power, and power alone. We worshipped the Emperor because he was powerful, and when he rebuked us, our glorious father went looking for something more powerful into which he could pour his love.'

The Anakatis swung again, its voice a drone in Layak's ear, speaking of what he could become if only he would take the weapon for himself.

Take the blade, the voice said. ***Build a new Monarchia in your own name, on the foundations of this city. Let its temples rise into the sky, let it stand as a bastion of faith, its towers proclaiming one name, night and day, until the galaxy comes to recognise you above all else. Zardu Layak! Not the messenger, but the message – a new god to lead the Pantheon.***

His right arm elongated with a crack, the bones breaking and re-forming in a few moments. They burst from beneath his muscles, piercing skin and blood-soaked ceramite alike. The bones formed spines, hard and sharp, rising from his wrist and hand – a fleshy mace, dripping with greasy ichor.

'I have been blessed with many gifts,' Layak said, as he punched his new fist into Hebek's stomach. The first blow only splintered the ceramite of his brother's armour, but the second and third reached the organs beneath. Layak found he could taste the older Space Marine's blood through his changed hand, the tang of copper and heat somehow playing across his tongue as his bone blades dug deep into Hebek's guts.

Hebek stumbled backwards, and Layak let him fall, the force of the impact showering dust from the ceiling above. The Anakatis blade fell with him – released by a loosened grip, it clattered against the stone, sending a discordant wail through the chamber. The thralls twitched at the sound, but did not halt their praying, the repetition of Hebek's name almost perverse as his blood mixed with the dust to create mud.

Layak let the blades recede into his wrist, bathing in the agony as the bones of his arm knitted together once more to form the standard human skeletal configuration. He shifted his gaze from his arm to the Anakatis blade, and to Hebek. The older Space Marine's wounds were grievous, but they would not kill him, and already, he had drawn himself to his knees.

He closed the distance between them slowly, stepping in pools of Hebek's dark blood. The blade seemed to quiver as he reached for it, and the eyes on its surface fixed him with unblinking stares. It was far older than his Legion, he knew – older even than humanity's first flight across the stars. A blade not made, but formed – a slash of malice, frozen in time. It was unique, but it was not the only blade of its kind, and it sang for its siblings.

He reached his fingers for it, and then he stopped.

'Take it,' Lorgar said.

Layak saw the towers rise into the white sky. A new ziggurat, grander than Hebek's own, its construction guided by his knowledge of a thousand civilisations.

And then he saw the towers topple and fall. Ruin came to the city, as ruin would come to all things. The echo of cruel laughter, as the gods of ruin cast down even the mightiest mortal works.

'I belong to the gods, and the gods alone,' Layak said,

Temptation released its grip on his hearts, and Lorgar smiled, showing a monster's teeth.

'Good,' he said. *'You have taken the first step.'*

The blade howled, denied its prize, and the chamber groaned in sympathy. The groan became a roar as shards of stone began to fall from the ceiling above.

Hebek knelt in the ruin of his stomach as the shards bounced from his shoulders.

For a moment, Layak was a boy again. Red light on blood-stained armour, crimson on crimson. A place of death. Of rebirth. A life remade, given purpose. The laughing giant, younger then, his hair still shot through with beams of black. An act of mercy.

'Help me...' Hebek said, the shower of rocks becoming a rain, then a deluge, as the ziggurat began to collapse in on itself.

A slab of stone the size of a Rhino tank dislodged from the ceiling, tumbling end over end towards Hebek's broken body. Layak threw his hand forward, two fingers describing a circle in the stinking air of the chamber, and pulled the slab away, letting it slam into the ground beyond the metal throne.

Layak ran towards his brother, dodging a chunk of roughly carved rock, before coming to rest with his shoulder against Hebek's. Blood painted the older Space Marine's chin the same deep red as his armour, but his eyes were still sharp. They fixed on Layak's now.

'You did not take the blade.'

From outside the city, it appeared that the world itself was collapsing. The ziggurat fell in on itself, its intricate construction undone, as if a central thread had been unpicked by an invisible hand. A terrible sound – rending, grinding, rumbling – rolled across the forest, shaking the ground that Barnhart and her dwindling troops defended, shaking the earth tens of kilometres into the distance.

Millions of tonnes of material fell upon the chamber at the ziggurat's centre, and yet the two brothers nestled within were not harmed. Layak held his concentration, bare hand shaking and nose bleeding with the effort, as he recited words of protection and beseechment. Each word was agony – his throat burned and his gums bled, tongue blackening with their corrupting meaning – but he spoke them perfectly, maintaining a sphere of grey smoke that enveloped them both.

Eventually, the cacophony subsided. The darkened ceiling of the chamber had become white, exposed to the sky as the rest of the structure collapsed into the network of tunnels that lay underneath its foundations, and Layak let the sorcery fall.

With an effort, he stood. He towered over the still-kneeling Hebek, a giant and a child, an inversion of their first meeting.

The older Space Marine's grey hair hung lank on his head, shiny with sweat. His chest worked, breathing hard, pulling dry air into his enhanced lungs. He looked to Layak and raised his arm, like he was trying to block out the sun.

'You saved me.'

Layak ignored the statement. He placed a boot on a fallen slab, and climbed it, turning his back on Hebek to look across the wreckage of another destroyed city.

'I thought I was mad, at first,' Layak said. 'After Monarchia, our father appeared to me in my dreams. So many of our brothers were shattered by the death of the Perfect City. I thought myself among them. But who was I to ignore the words of my primarch? So I listened to Lorgar, and I did as he asked. I hoarded the artefacts that we were sent to destroy. If madness was to be my fate, then so be it.

'I burned with shame. To keep my secret from my brothers in the Legion was hard. To keep it from my Ashen Circle – from Saucan, from Kulnar. From *you*. That nearly killed me.'

'Then why did you do it?' Hebek asked.

Layak took a deep breath, and felt his changed body. He felt his hearts beating in the galaxy's impossible rhythm. He felt his blood, hot and vital, pulsing in his veins and arteries. He felt muscles swelling and contracting, hard as ceramite.

And he felt changes beneath his skin: tendons and bones realigning, meat and metal growing together. He turned to Hebek.

'Because they will win,' Layak said. They were not words of exultation, and they left his mouth almost as a sigh. A cosmic truth, simply relayed. 'A thousand worlds, Hebek, we burned them together. A thousand civilisations, separated by unimaginable distances and thousands of years. Did you never stop to think why they feared the same shapes in the darkness? Why they – why we – create the same myths, no matter where we spread throughout the stars? The gods are real, Hebek, and they are inevitable. Chaos is inevitable.'

'How do you know?' Hebek asked, his voice faltering.

'Because I have seen it,' Layak said softly.

He laid a hand on Hebek's forehead. It was a gentle touch, but a jolt of agony coursed through the older Space Marine's body as Layak showed him what he was to become, what Terra would become, and what the galaxy would become.

Hebek twitched in response.

'Pain brings clarity,' Layak said.

The system's pale sun was setting, casting long shadows across the ruined city. The ziggurat had become a crater, like the impact point of some vast meteor, filled now with the shattered remnants of the monument. Layak dragged his brother from the centre of the crater, over rock slabs, pulling him upwards, steadily, into what remained of the light.

They looked out across the wreckage of the city together, breathing in unison for a moment, before Layak crouched next to the older Space Marine. The wind picked up, its effects no longer baffled by the once-vast structure, and it whipped at Hebek's long hair, pulling it back from his face.

Lorgar stood in front of the brothers.

'Do you see?' Layak asked.

Hebek followed his brother's gaze. 'I do. I understand now.'

Their father shone in the setting sun, an aura of gold like a halo around his head. As they watched, his fingers worked, and broken stone rose from the earth, shards of rock from the broken ziggurat rising again. They lifted and swirled together, locking and interlocking, until they formed a gate of ochre that framed Lorgar and the setting sun behind him.

'Step through,' Lorgar said.

'I cannot take the blade,' Layak said to Hebek. 'It has to be you.'

Layak flicked his hand, and, despite his injuries, Hebek stood. Blood pumped from the hole in the Word Bearer's stomach as Layak controlled his brother's body like a puppet, guiding him to kneel in the shattered stone, thrusting his hands between broken slabs to find his quarry.

He succeeded. Hebek pulled the Anakatis blade from where it had fallen, and raised it high in the growing darkness.

Hebek turned the blade in his hands, placing the hilt against the ground, the point against his chest.

'The blade is only the instrument, you see. It is the act that holds the power. I thought I had been brought here for the Anakatis, but I am here for *you*, Hebek, for what you and our brothers represent.'

Hebek spoke between wheezing breaths. 'Why send us away, just to kill us?'

Layak put his forehead to Hebek's.

'Because I was weak,' he whispered. 'I was weak, like you, and I showed mercy. I will not make that mistake again.'

Layak twisted his hand, and Hebek gasped as his synapses exploded with pain, quickening the beat of his hearts, and sending blood torrenting from the wound in his stomach.

'Where is Kulnar?' Layak asked.

'He… does not want to be found,' Hebek said, through gritted teeth. Layak folded his fingers into a fist, and the flesh of Hebek's throat began to bubble and swell, agony twisting his very cells. When he spoke, his voice was strangled.

'In the north! He is in the north. He found something up there. He is a scholar, always searching.'

'And Saucan?'

'I don't know. He disappeared soon after we arrived. Too restless. Too angry.'

'The mountain,' Layak said. He saw it through the gate, once more, one amongst many. 'He is beneath the mountain. I have seen it in my dreams. I will find it.'

Hebek raised his head, his body suspended by sorcery and the Anakatis blade pressed against his chestplate. His hair hung limp, thick with sweat and blood.

'It could have been yours,' Hebek wheezed. His breathing was shallow now. 'But it wasn't enough, was it?'

'No,' Layak said, simply.

Hebek wheezed a laugh. 'It never will be.'

The sun finally set over the horizon, and Lorgar disappeared. Darkness filled the gate.

A part of Zardu Layak, buried deep in a memory, wanted to speak.

I'm sorry.

'Mercy is weakness,' he said, instead. He gestured, and Hebek slumped forward, impaling himself on the Anakatis blade.

Zardu Layak felt part of himself die.

Agony torched his nerves as his soul was sheared, but beneath his helmet, his mouth split into a smile, revealing fangs in a darkened maw.

The long-legged thing clawed at the veil between realities until a thousand deaths cut a hole large enough for it to slip through. It found itself on the other side, in a world of solidity, of touch, and blood, and pain, and death. Its nose twitched, and its tongue lashed at the air, tasting for the first time. It liked the taste of this world.

Its eyes saw reality in smears of colour – souls as flickering lights, their strength described by their intensity. Excitement was beyond its simple understanding, but it relished its new existence, aching to taste pain and anguish, misery and sadness. It took a moment to drink that anticipation in, long, clawed legs clicking on yellow stone.

Another soul, cast out of its own body, found the soulless thing before it could begin its new life. They were poor fits, really, but nature abhors a vacuum, and the cast-out soul found itself falling into its new form.

It was a stretched, strained thing, built for hauntings and nightmares, but it was a body. It could not go back to its first body, not after what had happened. The soul moved its new limbs gingerly, getting the measure of them, walking on clawed feet and using its hands as balance. It tried to speak, but its jaws were not built for human words, and a hiss came out instead. It would keep trying.

Dasich Shaav tried to open his eyes, and saw the world in a different light.

PART TWO

DUBITATIO

CHAPTER FOUR

It had been a storehouse once, Kulnar guessed, or some spartan hab-block, home to the people who lived and worked loading and unloading the ocean vessels at port. It was naught but ruins now. The ferrocrete remains stabbed into the indigo sky like broken teeth, black on dark blue.

Places had power, Kulnar knew. His was a Legion that raised temples and monuments, but for this purpose, the location did not matter. There did not need to be any history, no tyrants deposed or blood spilled. All that was needed was the circle, and the six figures who stood inside it. They stood as statues, their grey armour and their stillness rendering them almost invisible in the darkness. They were framed only by the rain that spattered from their armour.

Kulnar stopped at the edge of the circle and knelt. He touched two fingers to the edge of the circle, and they came away blackened. He ran them across his breastplate, tracing a circle on the painted ceramite. Keeping his head low, he spoke.

'Brothers of Ash. I mark myself with the purity of flame.'

Six voices rose in unison.

'We witness your absolution.'

Kulnar rose to his feet.

'Brother Kulnar,' one voice said. 'You may enter.'

Kulnar stepped across the ashen circle and smiled under his cowl. For all of the Word Bearers' mysticism, his Legion could be amusingly literal in its interpretations.

'Ashen brother,' he was greeted.

'Ashen brothers,' he responded, inclining his head to each in turn. They wore dark hoods in place of their helms, and the markings scored into their plate – individualised to the warrior – were all but invisible in the dark, but Kulnar could identify to whom he spoke easily enough.

Ko-Farak, hunched, his muscled shoulders heaving with each breath. Xol, his augmetic eye shining a dull red under his cowl. Saucan, taller than the others, but not yet in command. His time would come, Kulnar knew. The Legion was changing, and ambitious men could go far.

'Have you made your selection?' Ko-Farak asked.

'I have,' Kulnar said.

'Speak the name, so that we may stand in judgement.'

He did as he was bade, letting the name slip into the darkness.

Saucan spoke first, as Kulnar had expected.

'The boy?' he asked.

'A brother of the Legion,' Kulnar corrected.

'The boy,' Saucan persevered, with a sneer in his voice. 'The Chapter of the Ochre Gate can field some of the finest brothers in the Legion. Why him?'

'Because he is a powerful warrior,' Kulnar said, meeting the void where Saucan's face should have been. 'He is quick and strong, and decisive on the field of battle.'

'Our Chapter has many good warriors,' Ko-Farak said. 'What makes him worthy of a place amongst the circle?'

Kulnar raised his face to the sky, and tasted rain on his tongue. There was a faint tang of fyceline in the water. A sliver of truth.

'He has something missing. A void in his heart. Brotherhood alone does not satisfy him.' Kulnar let his face fall, and met the eyes of his brothers in turn. 'He will burn the galaxy to fill that void.'

When he stepped from the circle some time later, the rain had stopped. Two suns were rising over the ruined port, illuminating a sea thick with corpses. Kulnar offered a tight smile to the sunrise, and made his way back to the Thunderhawk. He had to welcome the man who would become Zardu Layak to the ranks of the Ashen Circle.

Zardu Layak knelt in the ruins of the city, and pulled a shawl from the leather pouch at his waist. It was old, and he opened it carefully, laying its eight corners down one at a time on a chunk of fallen stone. Inside were a handful of bones, and with his left thumb and forefinger he carefully collected them from inside the fabric. He closed his hand over them and prayed, blessing them with benedictions that he had learned from the teachings of Erebus and Lorgar.

They were small things, and only some were identifiable. He knew that there was a knuckle of a human finger, and part of a man's rib, but others were stranger objects. Carved or grown, he did not know – he had taken them from so many different worlds, from so many different creeds. It did not matter where they came from. It only mattered that they had power.

The practice was called sortilege, though it had other names. He knew at least ten, recorded in the texts that he had taken from the worlds he had razed. The method was always the same, though. Humans, separated by millennia and the infinite void, discovered that by asking the right questions and casting lots, they might find truth.

He cast the bones, letting them fall where they chose. An act of apparent randomness, but of course, it was not random. The gods spoke through the bones, and they answered his question. The bones lay across words and inscriptions in a myriad of languages and scripts, the books of Lorgar and the gospels of Erebus, and older texts, written in hieroglyphs and cuneiform.

They gave him the answer.

Hebek watched silently, the first Anakatis blade in hand, as Layak stood.

'I have found him.'

His brother. His next quarry.

Barnhart tracked the man with her lasgun. He was running in a headlong sprint, legs pumping, arms flailing, his human body pushed to its limits. Still, his face showed none of the effort, pulled as it was into the same rictus grin as the hundreds around him. She had killed dozens that day, but for some reason she found herself considering this man – who he'd been, what he wanted, why he was here, caked in filth, so desperate to throw away his life. She shook her head, blinked away the thoughts. She sighted her weapon as she had been taught, and – as she had countless times already – squeezed the trigger.

The weapon responded with an apologetic whine. She cursed, and called out.

'Adalwin, power pack!'

She placed her hand behind her back to receive the ammunition, and waited for the reassuring weight in her palm. None came. She clicked her fingers, called again, and when that did nothing, she risked turning her back on the battlefield to find out what was going on. Adalwin lay behind her, a neat circular hole scored in his forehead. Grey smoke wisped from the wound.

Barnhart scrambled backwards, keeping her head low to avoid the sporadic las fire from the horde, and scanned the muddy forest floor for a full power pack. She pulled one, two, three to her face, glancing at the readout on each. All empty. She cursed again, and looked down the makeshift defensive line. A handful of her soldiers stood against wooden barricades built hurriedly from fallen trees. Many others lay on the ground, their lifeless limbs thrown out to unnatural angles. Those who remained were running out of ammunition, too. She could tell by the sound. The comforting burr of outgoing las fire had gone, replaced by staccato blats of single shots. Some of her soldiers had been luckier, and picked up lasguns from fallen comrades. Others reached for laspistols holstered at their belts, their smaller payloads joining the barrage moments later. Those who could find no usable weapon filled the vox with their own calls for assistance, their voices increasingly panicked.

She pulled her own laspistol. Ditmar had given it to her, and it was an ornate thing, inscribed with symbols and inscriptions. Some of her soldiers had explained that the markings had come from a book that had been written by senior Astartes, but when she looked at them, they made her feel uneasy. She hated the weapon, but she had learned many decades ago that any gun was better than no gun.

Barnhart lifted the pistol and chose a target. Her eyes fell on the man again, amongst the throng. He was closer now. Close enough that she could see the unit patch on his mud-stained jumpsuit. She put his centre mass in the little pistol's sights, and squeezed the trigger.

At the same moment, a las bolt fizzed past her ear, close enough that she felt its heat on her skin. Her ankle stuck in the thick mud as she jerked away from the projectile, and she fell, twisting around to land next to Adalwin's corpse. She could smell cooked meat. She tried to rise, but couldn't get traction on the mud, and succeeded only in flipping herself into a seated position. Over the barricade, she could see the man, leading the charge of a larger group. His makeshift cleaver was crude and rusted, but its edge glittered in the fading light.

Barnhart keyed her vox. 'All squads, fall back in ranks. Conserve ammunition, priority targets only.'

The laspistol was half-embedded in the thick mud, and when she pulled it out, she could no longer see the inscriptions. She wiped as much as she could from the weapon. The man reached the barricade and jumped. He hit the lip of the metal barricade with his chest, knocking air from his lungs and blood from his mouth. Pink spittle splashed across Barnhart's flak armour, the same mixture of blood and saliva that foamed at the corner of his smiling mouth. He leapt again, his jerking, frantic motions more like the movements of a marionette, as if his body was being puppeted by some other power. He half-crawled, half-climbed over the barricade, slithering down the other side to the mud below, before leaping to his feet. He locked eyes with Barnhart, and pulled his cleaver into an overhead grip, ready to bring it down on her skull.

She raised the laspistol, squeezed the trigger with her tired trigger finger. The weapon clicked and whined. She squeezed again, and when that elicited the same response, she hurled the gun at the man's head. It hit him in the jaw, splitting his smiling lips. He did not even blink. He stepped forward, and she tried to keep her distance, backpedalling in the mud as she tried to draw herself to her feet. Her boots slipped in the muck, churned as it had been by the footfalls of her own soldiers.

'I'm sorry.'

The man stumbled and dropped the cleaver. It fell between her feet, rusted blade burying itself in orange mud. The man joined it, falling to his knees and clutching at his head. A sound rose from inside him: a feral groan of pain, of awful realisation. He looked at her, the smile finally fallen from his face, replaced by abject horror. His eyes brimmed with tears, and they spilled down his cheeks, carving lines in the dried mud on his face.

'What have I done?' he asked. His crying eyes pleaded for an answer, but Barnhart could not give him one. He sobbed – a strangled sound – and reached for the cleaver. Barnhart watched as he hefted the weapon with two hands, flipping the blade so that it was aimed at his own head. For a moment, she thought to stop him, but mercy had left this place. He met her eyes once more as he slammed the cleaver into the centre of his own skull, splitting his forehead in two. Blood joined tears as the man slumped face-first in the mud.

There was a rumble in the distance, like the sound of distant engines. It grew in strength, until the trees shook, then the ground itself. Barnhart stared in horror as the tower of the ziggurat toppled. It fell achingly slowly at first, and then all at once, as the tower brought the rest of the structure down with it. The sun appeared behind the ziggurat, its absence brightening the forest, until it was blotted out by a plume of dust that rose into the sky like a volcano without eruption.

The city's collapse was a turning point. Whatever connection the attacking mass had was now severed. They were a mass no longer, but thousands of individuals, holding their heads in some combination of shock, disbelief, and horror. Some joined the man with the cleaver. Bereft, they turned their weapons on themselves, ejecting las bolts into their own brainpans, or piercing their hearts with makeshift blades. Others simply stood in place, or fell to their knees, eager for the earth to swallow them whole, to take them back to the dirt.

Barnhart touched her vox again, preparing to send a message to her troops, but before she could, the device crackled. The voice on the other end was deep and mellifluous.

'Lieutenant Barnhart. Prepare your troops. We travel north.'

Layak had not been alone when he had rendezvoused with the Children of the Blessed Moon. Another of his number had joined him as well: a hulking figure in broken red armour, who followed Layak around like a shadow. His breastplate was rent open, Barnhart noticed, a jagged hole in the armour at an angle that made it look like a predator's smile. Like Layak, he wore a helmet, but his was of a different pattern, with eye-lenses that glowed a dull green – the colour of bog ghosts. He carried a monstrous blade that appeared more like a remnant from some xenos creature than a weapon crafted by human hands, studded as it was with teeth and horns.

She remembered Jassim, remembered the man's brainless corpse, animated by Layak's dark powers to speak and to lead. Possibilities and potentials unspooled themselves in her mind. She shut them down with a force of will. The truth was less important than survival.

Only twenty of her soldiers remained. She had no time to bury the others. The lucky ones lay in one piece – others had been hacked to death by the thralls, arms and legs strewn across the forest floor. An uncountable number of their attackers had joined them in death, killed either by las bolt or by their own hand, turning their weapons upon themselves as the city – and their collective compulsion – collapsed.

The survivors only half-filled one compartment of the lander. Palgen and Ditmar were among them, the latter now tasked with maintenance of the dead Adalwin's comms array. The big man looked like a child as he adjusted the dials on the front of the device, lost in complexities he did not fully understand. None of them dared look towards the front of the vessel, and the compartment that contained Layak and his hulking companion.

Barnhart took the controls and the craft lifted off from the forest floor, angling north. Layak had scanned geopositional data relayed from *The Path Less Travelled*, and provided a new target: the ruins of a city in the planet's north, far beyond the boundary of its polar ice cap.

The scenery changed beneath the lander, the orange and green of the mud forest giving way to the dappled grey of tundra, and then the pristine white of snowfields.

'My lord,' she asked Layak, after she had engaged the lander's limited autopilot functionality. His grey helm swivelled to regard her, its blank expression unreadable. Her question almost caught in her throat, but if she was to die, she wanted to go to her grave with an answer. 'If I may... Why did you choose my unit for this mission? Standard protocol sees Space Marines serving alongside their brethren, not so... close to members of the mainline forces.'

A single red eye-lens bored into her like a dying sun, and she fought the urge to look away.

'I understand your unit has a reputation for particular... devotion,' Layak said. 'Perhaps that caught my attention.'

'Thank you, my–'

'Or perhaps you were lost between assignments. A sweep of a pen here, a misfiled document there, and you drop out of sight. A rounding error. A resource that would not be missed.'

'I...' Barnhart stuttered.

'But I believe something else. Would you like to know what I believe, Lieutenant Barnhart?'

It was cold in the lander, but a bead of sweat coalesced, before tracing the length of her back. 'Yes, my lord,' she answered.

'I believe you are here because the gods will it.'

She saw the city's spires through the viewport before the autopilot announced their approach. They rose from the ice like spears cast down by an angry god, silver in the moonlight. The cold licked against the drop-ship, trying to get in, leaving webs of frost across its armaglass panels.

They touched down at the edge of the city, and the bitter cold hit her like a gut punch as soon as the craft's ramp opened. Barnhart had fought on such battlefields before, had seen men and women die on the ice. The cold did strange things to a corpse, the normal biological processes of decomposition slowed to a crawl. The creatures that normally feasted on the softer parts of the human animal – insects and bacteria – could not thrive in such a place, so corpses kept their eyes, the orbs frozen blue, staring into the white for seasons upon end.

Barnhart followed Layak onto the ice, and wondered if this was where she would die.

CHAPTER FIVE

The shape of a city remained, but it was a city no more. There had been great buildings, towers of silver and stone, but they had been smashed apart by some ancient cataclysm, and then worn away by millennia of harsh weather – a quick wound, and then a slow death. Many of them had been part-buried by snow, their foundations hidden beneath drifts of pure whiteness.

Barnhart was already cold in the snowstorm, but the uncanny city had dug out an icy pit in her stomach that made her shudder. Layak led the way. The Space Marine moved at the head of the pack like a predator, stopping at crossroads in the ruined streets and turning his head, as if he was picking up a scent, before moving off again, his massive boots barely making a sound on the ice. She led her squad in his wake, trying to keep to the cover-and-advance strategies she had learned during her training, setting firing arcs and scanning what remained of the city's doorways for targets. The place had been abandoned centuries before – maybe even millennia – and yet she felt eyes upon her, as if the city itself was watching.

'We need to get out of here, lieutenant,' Palgen said, under her breath.

Barnhart wanted to agree with her sniper, to lead her troops back to the lander and leave this grave site to be buried by the endless snow. She turned, just for a moment, to look back at the way they had come. She met the green eyes of the silent warrior instead. Layak had tasked him with bringing up the rear of their small force, and he had obeyed without question. Where Layak padded, he trudged, his cruel blade carving a furrow through the snow as he dragged it behind him.

'Quiet,' she snapped back. She wanted to rebuke her further, to exert her authority as de facto leader of what remained of the Children of the Blessed Moon, but movement caught Barnhart's eye. Just a flicker, white against the white snow, gone as fast as it had come. She snapped her laspistol up, narrowing her eyes to see better in the cold, but saw only blue-white ice and the steadily falling snow. Her body and mind had been pushed to breaking point. Perhaps she was going mad.

Another flash of movement.

'Lord Layak,' she called. 'I think we are being followed.'

The Space Marine turned. The plates of his grey armour were rimed with frost.

'We are,' he said. 'It has followed us from the forest.'

'What is it?' Barnhart asked.

'It is Shaav.'

Layak had released soul-seekers – creatures from beyond the veil drawn to the living – into the city first, and he had scoured it himself. But even after a day of searching, of Kulnar there had been no sign, only the whistle of the polar wind, and the crack of ice underfoot – the grave of a civilisation long forgotten.

The bones had lied. Wherever his brother was now, he was not here.

He would move on, leave this place to the ice and snow, let them bury it forever. He would find the mountain he had dreamt of. He was already strong.

The wind spoke with Lorgar's voice, reminding him of his path.

'You are not ready.'

Layak took a breath to calm the frustration boiling in his chest. He closed his eyes and let the polar air reach his lungs, cold and cleansing.

When he opened them again, a structure rose before him. Layak had passed by it before on his search through the city, but this time he noticed its differences. It was circular in shape, taller and far wider than the ruins around it, and somehow less affected by the erosion of the passing millennia. Its outer walls were frozen, but still intact, with open gates placed at regular intervals along their length. A place for the people of this city, Layak surmised, a collective meeting place, perhaps.

He paused in front of the nearest gate, and stepped through.

The gate brought him through a tunnel that baffled the wind, before opening out onto a circular field of snow and ice, wide enough to land a Thunderhawk. Layak looked up and saw snowfall, but erosion had not collapsed this structure's ceiling – it had been built with no roof. Stairs remained, worn but still usable, leading to second, third, and fourth floors, each smaller than the last, and each looking out across the central space.

'A place of knowledge,' Lorgar said. The primarch stood in the open area, close to a raised dais that marked the centre of the structure. In common with the walls, it was built from stone – smooth, and unadorned – like the base of a statue that may once have stood in the ancient city. Snow fell from the sky above, and its flakes did not settle upon the primarch's massive shoulders.

'The bones lied,' Layak said, his frustration not yet truly calmed. 'Kulnar is not here.'

'We see what we want to see. Look again.'

'My seekers cannot find him. *I* cannot find him. He is nothing. An old man. Unworthy of our attention.'

'He stands in your path. You must walk it to its conclusion. You must be cleansed.'

'Let me find the mountain you showed me, let me finish this. I am ready.'

'You are not!'

Lorgar's golden eyes flashed black as his words reverberated from the walls of the structure. The ice and snow fell away, just for a moment, and Layak stood amongst the flames of a firestorm. The city burned, its very sky on fire.

And then it was gone, replaced by the serenity of the snowfield.

Silence, and then Lorgar spoke again.

'Open your eyes.'

Layak stared at his surroundings, looking for something that would give a clue to Kulnar's location. A wall ran in a circle around the snowfield, and he moved to it, crunching snow and cracking ice beneath his tread as he walked. He touched the wall with his bare hand, trying to glean some meaning from this place. A susurrus fell from his lips, whispered prayers to call forth the memories ingrained in the stone of this place.

'It was... a library for the beings of this place,' Layak said. 'I can feel the echoes of their understanding. They learned things here, incredible things, but...'

He felt a jolt of pain travel the length of his arm, and smiled as it lit his nerves ablaze. Pain always brought clarity.

'They could not find the answers they sought.'

A cracking sound broke the cold silence, and Layak turned. From beneath the snowfield, a huge figure was emerging, pulling itself from its resting place under the layers of ice at the centre of the open-air library. Its body was swollen and misshapen, with lumpen flesh – sickly blue with cold – protruding from rents in ceramite armour.

It carried the chainsword of a line legionary, wielded in two hands. As it pulled itself fully from its grave, Layak saw its face: green eyes, their light ghostly behind a Mark IV helmet, its faceplate cracked along the cheek, exposing skin, loose and sallow. Its pauldron bore the icon of the XVII Legion.

'To me!' Layak called, summoning the Children of the Blessed Moon and Hebek into the library, but not before the swollen Word Bearer closed the distance between it and Layak, swinging its chainsword in a low arc.

He raised a leg and stamped on the chainsword, trapping the whirling blade under his boot. The teeth dug helplessly into the ground, churning permafrosted earth with a mechanised growl, as the figure stumbled forward, off balance. Layak used the momentum, and stabbed his axe-rake into the ribs of the massive warrior, letting it settle between the segmented armour before he gunned the motor. Chunks of meat and ceramite gouted from the wound it created, spraying across the snow.

Layak squeezed the weapon's trigger, digging deeper into flesh and bone, waiting for the scream. None came. He looked up into the warrior's green eyes just in time to take a clubbing blow across the side of his skull. The force of the impact punched Layak into the air, and sent him crashing to the frozen ground. The hulking warrior pulled its chainsword free from the earth, moving with elephantine strides in his direction.

Las bolts peppered its flank, cauterising wounds where they hit swollen flesh. Barnhart's remaining troops took aim as they sprinted through the gates and into the library's circular central area, setting up firing positions around its perimeter, and pouring volleys of las fire onto the creature. It barely registered the impacts, insensate to the pain of its body being burned away, its focus turned only to Layak.

Black flame was coalescing in Layak's palm as a second crack, then a third, reached his ears. Two more bloated monstrosities in broken armour clawed their way from the ice, green light dancing in their eyes. One carried a chainsword of the same pattern as the first; the other hefted a bolter, which it raised with one hand, firing from the hip.

Layak hurled the black flame forward, but – the incantation rushed and incomplete – it fizzled in the air and fell short of its target. Fast as thought, Layak used two fingers to draw a circle, and bolter shells that had been arrowing for his chest caromed away, sorcery redirecting them into the structure's walls. A series of nearby detonations were met with screams. At least one of the bolts had bisected Children of the Blessed Moon.

The creature reloaded the bolter to fire again, but it would not have the opportunity – Hebek appeared at Layak's side, bringing his Anakatis blade in a diagonal cross that cut straight through the bolter's barrel, down into its magazine. The ammunition exploded, the force of it annihilating the creature's forearm, shredding flesh and bone to the elbow. In a living body, such an injury would have meant a shower of gore, but no blood sprang from the wound, any fluid in the thing's body having been frozen solid long ago.

Hebek brought the Anakatis blade – unaffected by the explosion – around, aiming a violent thrust towards the second creature. It parried the strike with its chainsword, surprisingly nimble in its motions, and brought the whirring blade across Hebek's chest. Monomolecular-edged teeth bit into the already broken ceramite of his breastplate, and into the skin below. Once more, Layak expected gore, and once more, none gouted from the wound.

The heat of las fire refocused Layak's attention, just as the one-armed creature barrelled into him, knocking him from his feet. He hit the ice hard and rolled, coming up with black fire in each palm. Able to complete his incantation this time, he let each flame grow until gobbets of burning, stinking poison ran between his fingers and hissed against the icy floor, before flinging them at the creature. The fireballs slammed against its stomach, where they caught, the insidious fire burning through the creature's belly to the organs below.

Silent but for the bubbling of melting flesh and the crackle-pop of flame, the creature still stumbled towards Layak. Calling the warp's venom forward, Layak threw fireball after fireball at it, until it was a walking pyre, what remained of its skin sloughing off as the once-frozen muscles beneath were cooked. It fell forward onto its face, flames still roaring as they used the last of its corpse as fuel.

Satisfaction was replaced by pain as Layak's shoulder exploded. He turned his head, and saw the whirring teeth of a chainsword at his cheek, the weapon having been shoved through his shoulder blade to punch out of his collarbone. He spun to face his attacker, ripping the chainsword from the first creature's hand with the force of the turn. It reached for him with its hands instead, and found purchase with its stubby fingers around his helmet.

Ceramite cracked as the thing squeezed, and Layak's vision narrowed, his skull bearing the pressure. He fell backwards, and the thing came with him, its vice grip carrying them both towards the dais at the centre of the space. Layak felt his back impact the stone, and tried to pull the thing's hands off his head. He could hear las bolts hitting it from behind, could feel the juddering impact of the superheated beams on its back, but it was relentlessly strong – like trying to pull an iceberg from an ocean.

He heard cracking, and realised it was his own skull. Layak

gritted his teeth, bearing the pain, and instead used it to change his body. The bones of his hands broke and lengthened, agony giving him the strength for metamorphosis, nails becoming diamond-hard claws that dug – slowly – through the creature's face, piercing ceramite first, then skin, skull, and the frozen mind beneath. Only when his two hands were deep inside the creature's skull did he pull them apart, splitting its head in two.

The creature wavered for a moment before slumping over him, its bulk pinning him in place against the dais. The chainsword still buzzed in his shoulder, loud and insistent. He gathered the strength to push the headless creature to the floor, and blood forced its way from the gaping wound in his shoulder, the flow finding its way between rubberised seals and ceramite plates to reach the frozen stone beneath. The warmth of it melted the ice, and as it touched stone, the dais responded.

A wave of golden light crossed the city, and in its wake, Layak saw the history of the city written on its walls. Symbols covered every surface still standing: words, runes, and pictures scraped into stone or etched into metal. Where they had not been carved, they had been daubed, painted onto walls, ceilings, and any other surface that remained by unseen artists.

Layak pulled the chainsword from his shoulder, and sat on the dais, gasping. His pain was changing his body still, knitting the bones of his shoulder faster than possible for a normal Space Marine. A skill. A gift.

He understood now the purpose of the place in which they stood. 'It was not a library,' he said, as he took in the symbols. 'This was a church. And this' – he laid a hand on the dais, the stone stained red with his blood – 'was an altar.' He was not the first sacrifice, he knew – their pain and their blood had brought knowledge. The power of sacrifice.

'You are right.'

Layak recognised the voice, still.

Kulnar stood in the snow before him. He wore the crimson of the Legion in its later years, but it had dulled in the cold, the edges rimed with frost. The Chaplain was diminished by his hardships as well. He appeared smaller, weaker, older, as if the icy wind had chipped away at the facade of the warrior and left only a husk, hardened and cold. But then Layak knew Kulnar, and that appearances could be deceiving with the man.

'Welcome to my sanctuary. Your arrival is written.' Kulnar gestured at the closest wall and the script scrawled on its surface, then cocked his head to the side, almost apologetically. 'Somewhere.'

There were shapes Layak recognised amongst the symbols, remembered from stone tablets and skin scrolls, words and runes that had been etched into metal and drawn in ink and blood. They were segments of truth, he knew, their universality proved by their presence having been shared between civilisations that grew in ignorance, light years apart. Profane shapes, marks of the gods and their lesser generals and courtesans.

But it was not enough. There were gaps in what he saw. Gaps in his own understanding, or gaps in the record itself, he did not know.

'What does it say?' Layak asked.

'It is a history. And a warning, and a promise. It is many things.'

'Xenos?'

'In a manner of speaking. They were certainly different to us. They found the blades on this world, and in the peace they brought, they studied. They studied for millennia – thousands of generations, turned to the questions of existence, of reality. Minds open, thoughts unsullied by conflict, or politics, or' – he tapped his own chest absent-mindedly – 'gene-bred loyalty.'

Snow fell from the white sky.

'They recorded it all, in the body of this city. Only the bones remain now, but I thought that would be enough.' His shoulders fell. 'But I cannot piece it together, no matter how hard I try. I have been here...' Kulnar banged the heel of his palm against the side of his head, as if trying to dislodge the information. He looked up at Layak. 'How long have I been here, brother?'

'Decades,' Layak said.

'Is that true? It feels longer. Or shorter? I confess, time does not have much meaning to me any more.' He turned back to the wall, and began tracing his finger along the script again. 'It must be here somewhere. Some configuration of words, of meaning...'

'What answer do you seek?' Layak asked.

'Oh, I already know the answer,' Kulnar said. 'It is the question that eludes me. The galaxy is full of answers for those who want them. But the right question, brother – that is the hardest thing to find.' He sighed and tapped a shape on the wall, once, twice, then traced a line to another, tapping it a final time. The air seemed to shimmer for a moment, and Layak felt his heartbeats slow. Snow that had been falling seemed to hang in the air, travelling its path to the ground with aching slowness. Layak looked back to Kulnar, and he saw that the Chaplain was facing him now, only five paces away.

'I wanted you to understand that, brother. Answers were never difficult for you, but you only ever had one question.'

The city moved. The church fell away, and ruined walls reassembled themselves, growing in height, closing themselves to the elements with ceilings. Spires and towers buried themselves, before bursting from the snow in new locations, with new shapes and different numbers of sides. Motion, unstoppable motion, as the city reconfigured itself around the two Space Marines, the student and the master. Across it all, the words danced like sprites of fire, rewriting themselves into beautiful verse, arcane truths, and maddening gibberish.

Until it stopped. The words settled into new homes, carved into ancient stone, and Layak and Kulnar stood in a temple, lit only by candlelight.

Layak reached for his axe-rake, and found the weapon's reassuring weight in his palm. He gunned the weapon once, listening for its animal purr.

Kulnar tilted his head. 'That question. Do you remember it?'

The man who would become Zardu Layak had met Kulnar in the vessel's library, as he had done countless times since joining the ranks of the Ashen Circle. Their meetings had been proposed by Kulnar, and Layak had assumed them a part of his ascension to the formation – a chance for the older Space Marine to offer spiritual advice and wisdom accumulated over his long years of service. Layak had never seen Kulnar in study with any of his brothers, though, the Chaplain seeming to prefer to spend his waking hours in silent study by himself.

As usual, he found Kulnar at the long wooden desk that ran down the centre of the library, surrounded by open books of all varieties: treatises on faith and fealty, histories of the Unification Wars, star charts and planetary maps. Starlight shone in through the large windows that exposed the void outside, the brightness of a thousand pinpricks of light augmented by the glow-globes on the desk. Such windows were common on Word Bearers vessels – their primarch had always held that the most effective study was conducted against the backdrop of creation.

The older Space Marine greeted him warmly, gesturing to a stool on the other side of the desk.

'Please, sit. Join me.'

Layak sat. Kulnar regarded him with a smile for a moment, before reaching into a pile of texts. He removed a book and examined it in the light, before sliding it along the polished wooden desk to Layak. It was small, and bound simply in fabric, without any inscription on the cover. Layak knew it immediately.

'Meditations on Belief,' *he said. 'We are to discuss Lorgar's own work?'*

'The words of our primarch,' Kulnar said. 'Who better to advise us in matters of the spirit?'

'Yes,' Layak said. 'Of course there is wisdom in Lorgar's words. But…' He paused, confusion pursing his lips. 'Every Word Bearer can recite this text from memory. What is left to say on the matter that has not already been said?'

Kulnar breathed deep, forcing the seeds of frustration from his body before they took root.

'Everything, brother. This is no training manual, no field primer. We are not Guilliman's mindless automatons, built to perform our duties with no thought to the nature of existence around us. We are built in our father's image, and our father knows that the question is as important as the answer. More so, sometimes.' He reached over the desk and tapped the book. 'Lorgar's words invite questions. Questions that his sons should ask. Must *ask.' Kulnar spread his hands, a gesture of openness. 'So,' he said. 'What would you ask?'*

'I would ask if we could study something new,' Layak said, unconvinced by his mentor's argument. He picked up the book anyway, and leafed uncaringly through its pages. His eyes scanned passages that he had memorised decades earlier.

'Then I will ask you a question,' Kulnar said. He leant forward, placing his forearms flat on the desk. They were free of the tattoos that adorned Layak's own skin. He lowered his voice, as if to whisper a secret. 'What does Lorgar say to you?'

Layak's face froze. He tried to make his eyes move, to finish the passage he was re-reading, but he could not take it in, could not recite the words that he knew so well. His answer, when it came, was put forward with studied nonchalance.

'Lorgar?'

'Yes,' Kulnar said, unmoved by Layak's affectation. 'Even before our father returned from his pilgrimage, I know he appeared to you

in your dreams. He has been a presence in your mind since Monarchia, decades ago. I know that he speaks to you, and I know what he now asks you to do.'

Heat and cold swirled in Layak's gut, physical manifestations of his shame. He had not told a soul about his visions. And yet, Kulnar was confronting him with their reality, in the heart of their shared home.

He couldn't deny it.

'How did you know?' Layak asked.

'You are not alone in receiving visions,' Kulnar said. 'Others are cursed to suffer the same affliction.'

'Cursed?' Layak asked.

'Is it not a curse, to know how all of this – how you – will end?'

Layak found he could not answer the question.

'Please,' Layak said, finally. 'Do not tell the others of my visions. They would think me mad.'

'Rest easy,' Kulnar said. 'Your secret will remain yours to keep.'

'Thank you,' Layak told him. And to himself, he asked the question he had asked so many times before.

Why me?

Barnhart had seen Layak collapse before the blizzard descended. It had come on so suddenly that it could be no natural phenomenon. The snow stung where it hit her bare skin, and she'd had to narrow her eyes to slits just to maintain her vision, darkening the world as she saw it.

She swung her laspistol left and right, looking for targets. She could only see a few metres in front of her face, but made out dark figures looming from the dense fog, shapes like phantoms from ghost stories. Their hair was long and lank, and their jaws hung open beneath dead eyes of white.

Barnhart fired her laspistol, and felt a small amount of her fear dissipate as the bolt carved through one phantom, turning it to powdery snow. She fired again, and a second ghost dissipated.

The wind moaned in response – a deep sound, almost human. It seemed to come from behind Barnhart.

It was not the wind. A figure, tall and impossibly thin, stepped from the fog. Standing, its arms hung down almost to its knees, but it moved in a partial crouch, walking on its knuckles for balance.

Its eyes were black, and its nose was flat, pallid skin stretched over a humanoid skull like a perversion of a man. Only its mouth did not appear as a facsimile of humanity – it was a ring of flesh, needle-sharp teeth arrayed in a circle around its edges.

She raised her laspistol, but the thing backhanded it away, catapulting it from her hand, its too-long arms covering the distance between them easily. It loomed over her, its leech's maw working, opening, surely to suck her blood. She waited for its bite.

The thing spoke.

'I... Shaav,' it said.

Tears froze in her eyes as she stared at the thing. Its nightmare face was pleading, somehow. It raised its hands, a gesture of appeasement.

'Dasich Shaav. I... help you. I help Layak.'

The voice was human, but it sounded wet and percussive, as if the owner was not used to making the sounds of speech.

Just looking at the thing turned her stomach, but she had no time for questions. Ghosts rose from the fog, and Barnhart dropped to her knees, reaching for her laspistol in the snow. She sighted the weapon on the closest phantom, but before she could pull the trigger, it burst. Barnhart's eyes widened – letting more of the stinging snow in – as more of the phantoms reached for Shaav, only to explode as if they too had been shot when they came within a few metres of him. Something about him – his wrongness – somehow had a lethal effect on the phantoms.

She stared into his empty eyes. A wave of revulsion swept her body, but she stayed her hand. Survival came first.

'How are you doing that?'

His mouth shaped again, the words stuck in his throat. He tapped his elongated skull instead, as if that was explanation enough, and then – when Barnhart's brow furrowed – spoke.

'I... power. Mind power. Think, and...'

He gestured, expanding his clawed fingers.

'They die.'

A psyker. She had served with sanctioned psykers before, and even their presence – trained, marshalled, controlled – had unsettled her. A wild psyker, their powers unchecked... No wonder she found him so repellent, even before the transformation that seemed to have ruined his body. Now, he was a monster.

'What did he do to you?' she asked.

'I Dasich Shaav,' he said, eyes dark as night. 'I still Dasich Shaav...'

Barnhart swallowed her disgust. 'You protect me, and I'll protect you, okay?'

Shaav nodded, a movement that appeared alien to his new body.

The phantoms that came for them crashed harmlessly against Shaav's projected aura, like waves against the shore, as they ran for their only salvation in such a place, to Zardu Layak.

Barnhart and Shaav reached the altar together, visibility so poor that they couldn't see the stone object until they were almost upon it. Layak lay across it, limbs splayed as if dead.

Shaav moaned – an eerie sound, even in the mausoleum city – and placed a long-fingered hand on the Space Marine's chest. It rose and fell with his breathing, and Shaav's mouth widened.

'Listen to me,' Barnhart said. 'If he dies, we die. We need to keep him alive.' Shaav nodded, and Barnhart took the sucking noises he made as an acknowledgement of the plan.

The remaining Children of the Blessed Moon joined them, and together, they turned their weapons against the blizzard, defending the slumbering giant in grey lying across the altar.

The temple's silence was split by the grinding howl of a chainblade. Layak swung his axe-rake as he ran at Kulnar, aiming for the Chaplain's collarbone, cutting where the ceramite of his armour was thinnest.

The axe-rake passed through the Chaplain as if he was made of air. Expecting an impact that did not come, Layak stumbled forward, off balance, as the image of Kulnar disappeared, guttering from existence as if he was a candle flame that had been snuffed out by a swirling breeze.

'I know why you have come,' Kulnar said. He spoke from behind Layak, and the younger warrior spun to face the voice.

'For the Anakatis blades,' Layak said, facing the Chaplain.

'That is a lie, brother. The blades are powerful, of course. The first people of this world thought they could bind them here, but...' Kulnar raised his palms, gesturing at the temple around them. 'That did not go according to plan.' He offered a wry smile. 'Fascinating weapons, truly. Easily as old as our species, and imbued with a belligerent power. They want to hurt, to control, to kill, and they are good at it. They have cut quite a wound across the history of this galaxy. But there are a thousand such powerful weapons, on forgotten worlds such as this,' Kulnar said. 'Why *this* world? Why *these* weapons?'

'It is the will of the gods. It is fate.' Layak reached out with his fingers, probing the edges of the veil for Kulnar's true form. He wanted to tear it, to rend it, but found only cold nothingness in the ether.

'Ah, fate,' Kulnar said. 'I will show you fate, brother.'

An eyeblink, and the temple was gone. Layak burst from the earth in a shower of snow, finding his footing in an open ice field, far from the city. He saw no sky, no horizon – the field seemed to exist in an empty plane. Still, wind whipped at his body, an unnatural cold he could feel through his armour.

Kulnar's voice carried on the wind. 'My brothers became frustrated at my study. They craved certainty, just as father did. Just as you did. But I knew one thing for certain – I could not let them leave me unprotected in this place as the others carved out their own fiefdoms. They would not let me study in peace, not with what I might learn. So I gave my brothers a gift. I took their doubt away.'

Five more giants crawled from the snow, pulling their malformed bodies from their frozen graves. Their armour was cracked and broken in places, exposing mutated flesh that spilled from ceramite in lumpen tumours.

'We are all searchers, Lorgar's sons, all yearners,' Kulnar said. 'It is his flaw, the taint in his blood that he passed to his sons. We came here together, and we found a truth, just as our father did. But in that truth, we found no absolution, just oblivion.'

Layak thought he saw Hebek amongst their number, or a version of the man. His Mark IV plate was broken and daubed in symbols, his body a swollen ruin.

'This is what becomes of those who give themselves to your gods. They become mindless creatures. Chattel beasts. Slaves to darkness.'

Layak rolled as a chainsword descended through the fog, and felt pain in his still-healing shoulder. He heard teeth shave ceramite, the hilt of the weapon close enough that he could feel the heat of its motor on the bare skin of his face. The warrior wielding the sword hung over him, and he kicked out at its shin, trying to break bone, or at least dislodge the Space Marine from its feet, but the blow had no effect – it was like kicking a frozen tree.

He fired his bolt pistol from the hip instead, and the rounds punched – one, two – through the lumpen skin that spilled out of the thing's broken breastplate. Layak heard the whump of detonation inside the body, muffled and wet.

The thing swayed on its feet, green eyes shimmering.

'I envy them,' Kulnar said. 'To be unburdened by knowledge. They are above questions.'

Layak pushed the blade slave with a flick of his wrist, the projection of force enough to topple it. It erupted into snow as it impacted to the ground, its massive frame disappearing into the white.

'More falsehoods,' Layak said, breathing hard. 'You denied them the truth. They serve you now, when they should serve the gods.'

'I admit, the gift I gave them served me well. I am selfish,' Kulnar said, in countless sighing voices. 'In this solitude, I have come to understand this about myself. I have twisted words and deceived brothers. I have altered events with a thought or gesture to serve my desires. To serve my truth – that I am not satisfied with the same questions that you are.'

'Weakness,' Layak hissed. 'You equivocate and hide behind questions, too scared to make a decision, and see the truth that father did – we serve the gods.'

'We are all weak. You may kill your past, you may take a new name, but still, at your core, part of your humanity remains. It always will, as long as you question. As long as a sliver of doubt lives in your heart.'

'I have no doubt,' Layak shouted. With a thought, he pulled at the ice below the closest blade slave, causing it to lose its footing.

'A lie. Even now, you question. Are you truly here?'

A rumble, and the ruined city rose from the once-featureless earth, its walls and buildings appearing as discarded bones on the floor of some dread predator's lair.

He was alone in its streets.

'Show yourself, Kulnar,' he called. 'Free me from this place, and face me.' His own words echoed back to him, reflected by the broken walls of the city.

Layak slowed his hearts, tried to let his frustration be carried away on the wind. He found a flicker of life in the dead city, and he spun, catching a glimpse of Kulnar in a shattered doorway. He raised his bolt pistol and fired. The mass-reactive shell sailed straight through the illusion, scattering snow as it continued into the sky, where it finally detonated. Layak wheeled and fired again, and another Kulnar-ghost dissipated in a puff of snow. His thermal sensors whirred, trying and failing to find red heat in the white cold. Layak snarled and pulled his helmet from his head, throwing it to the ground, where it buried itself in the snow. Cold hit his face like a backhand slap, already starting to freeze the spittle on his lips. He tasted the cold on a forked tongue, and searched in its thousand flavours for one.

+You cannot escape your doubt,+ Kulnar said in Layak's mind. +It is a prison. Just as this city will be.+

CHAPTER SIX

Layak focused on the ruined walls, on the script, trying to find a way to unbind Kulnar's sorcerous illusions, to find some meaning in this place. His careful probings at the veil became animalistic slashes, desperate attempts to bring himself back to reality, to escape the plane he had been transported to.

'The rulers of this city knew the power of the Anakatis,' Kulnar said. 'They valued wisdom, and they used the blade wisely, scholar kings ruling over a place of learning. I will show you.'

Layak found himself on a grand mezzanine that looked out over the ruined city, the apex of the tower scraping the base of the white clouds above. Despite the altitude, the wind had died away, and the snow that had swirled below was beginning to settle.

'They would observe their great work from this place,' Kulnar said. 'Their sorceries still have power today.'

Layak turned to find his brother walking from a chamber inside the tower. Unlike every other centimetre of the city, this tower's walls were pristine, the floor of the mezzanine laid in polished, unadorned marble.

'I find myself coming here more often in these times,' Kulnar continued. 'It really is quite beautiful.' He walked to the edge of the mezzanine and placed his hands on the stone balustrade that separated the Space Marines from the precipitous drop below. 'They would have seen the whole city from up here. I have seen glimpses of the place it must have been, but to see it in its prime...' He puffed out his cheeks. 'It would have been special. Perhaps even a rival of Monarchia.'

'Do not mention its name.'

'Another of my sins, brother – wistfulness. Sometimes I allow myself to believe that I will find my truth here. Some fundamental discovery that its rulers, even with generations at their disposal, did not find.' Kulnar sighed.

'The gods are the answer you seek.'

Kulnar's weary face broke into a smile. Sad, but warm, even in such cold.

'I failed you, brother. I tried to show you beyond the black and white, beyond the true and false. You read Lorgar's texts, but you never understood them.'

He considered the Anakatis.

'You have not come for the blade,' Kulnar said at last. 'You have come here for me. For what I am to you.'

'And what are you?'

'I am your questions, and I am your logic. I am part of your soul. I am your doubt.'

They met under a blazing sun. It hung in the void above Belief's Reward as the ship remained in orbit around the star's first world. The planet below was hot – hotter even than Colchis – and its sand was still being scrubbed from Zardu Layak's armour by Legion-serfs.

Kulnar laid a hand on the book that Layak carried, and slipped it from his grasp. He opened it to a central page and let his eyes run across the script. Layak fought the urge to grab it back. He wanted to keep the book close to him.

'What do you make of it?' Kulnar asked, not looking up while he read.

The younger Space Marine weighed his answer. What did he make of it? What did he make of the revelation that there were powers beyond comprehension in the galaxy? That they grew powerful through worship, through the exercise of their very nature? That countless human generations were right, and that the Emperor was wrong?

It was shattering. So fundamental in its wrongness, counter to everything that he had been taught, everything that he had been bred to be.

And yet. In his body, in his soul, he knew that he believed the words contained within. He had seen them before, in other configurations – in the texts he had hoarded and read, in secret shame, away from his brothers. They had never been so clearly explained, so well defined – a treatise on belief as a science, as the only recourse in a galaxy built on the very foundation of faith, as tangible and real as atoms.

What did he make of it?

It was the truth.

'Who wrote it?' he asked.

Kulnar closed the book with a snap, and looked up. 'Lorgar did.'

Layak's eyes widened. 'Lorgar wrote this?'

'Yes, my young friend.'

Reality seemed to lurch as Layak grappled with the enormity of the revelation. Events slotted into beautiful order, giving a life of apparent randomness meaning. The dreams of his father, the burden of preserving heresy, the despair of Monarchia – these were trials. His elevation to the Ashen Circle, mercy on the orbital of his birth, his new talents – these were his rewards. Lorgar wrote this. Lorgar, in his wisdom, in his faith. Lorgar, choosing to test him, even before his brothers were ready to see the truth.

A great cosmic machine showed itself to the man who would become Zardu Layak, and in that moment, its pistons and gears rotated into place. Tears filled his eyes.

Kulnar continued.

'Our father returned from his pilgrimage with this tome in hand. I believe he plans to disseminate copies amongst his sons – those whom he deems ready to receive such wisdom.'

'You were chosen?' Layak asked, managing to speak.

'I... acquired a copy,' Kulnar said, with a wistful smile. 'You know me, brother – if there are texts to be read, I will find them.' He waved the closed book in his hand. 'This is but a primer, in truth. Our father still adds to his opus, as he uncovers more about the galaxy. More about these gods.'

'Do you believe?' Layak asked. The words were already a test of the new faith.

'I... don't know,' Kulnar said, with disarming sincerity. 'Father truly believes, that much is obvious. But I have seen many things beyond my understanding, and have searched for meaning in all of them.' He tapped the book. 'I am yet to find a single answer that satisfies me.'

Anger flared in Layak's breast, unexpected. The heat of it surprised him, and he spoke with more venom than he intended.

'What if it is the truth?' he asked.

'What if it is not?' Kulnar countered.

In a flash, Layak grabbed the book back, wrenching it from Kulnar's grip in a moment of violence. He couldn't bear the thought of such beauty in the hands of one who didn't appreciate it.

'This is a blessing,' Layak said. 'Our father has given us a gift. A new future that we can work towards. A new truth.'

'Whose truth?' Kulnar asked, with a smirk. It was the smirk he used when he'd caught his protégé in an intellectual trap, and Layak hated it.

'Truth is truth,' Layak snapped.

Kulnar sighed, and let the vitriol hang in the air. It dissipated slowly, draining from the younger Space Marine like blood from a cut vein.

'The galaxy has always been black and white to you, brother,' the Chaplain said finally, with a chuckle. 'Look up. What do you see?'

Layak breathed deep, and tilted his head back. The void stretched above Belief's Reward, an endless ocean of black.

'Darkness,' Layak said.

'There is darkness,' Kulnar conceded. 'The dark of the firmament. And light, too – the blazing light of the suns that illuminate it. But there are so many shades of colour in the spaces between.'

'What is your point?'

'Truth is only truth from a perspective, brother. I hope you will come to see that.'

Layak considered the stars above, and, for the first time, saw shades of colour in the spaces between.

'I do not need questions,' Layak spat. 'I know the truth!'

'Or did you find a convenient lie?' Kulnar replied. 'You were desperate for something to cling to, some shred of meaning in a life shattered.'

'You know nothing!'

'I know all too well how you felt, brother. I was broken, too. To live with the pain of Monarchia, of our Legion's chastisement, of our father's abandonment, of our betrayal of our very reason for existence.'

'We exist to serve powers greater than ourselves.'

'And so we seek absolution. Our fathers abandon us, so gods must control us, because we cannot countenance the idea that it is ourselves – us! – in command of our destiny.'

'This is a test,' Layak said. 'This is all a test – a test of my faith, of my belief. My life has been a trial. Why else would I have suffered so? To live with such pain, such misery. The gods have tested me, and I have passed each test. This is but the latest, as I become their vessel.'

'All live in pain, brother,' Kulnar replied. 'Your experience is not so different from a trillion other souls. We were created for a purpose, our father was created for a purpose. We cannot understand a purposeless universe.' He offered a tight smile to the city below. 'But we exist in a grand confluence of events. We are but a moment in a history that has existed before us, and will far outlive us – just as this city will. A decision here, a word there, and a corner of the picture is illuminated by those who cannot see the full image. The work of gods, brother, or the randomness of an uncaring galaxy?'

'Impossible,' Layak spat back, frustrated. 'I have seen their power. I have *felt* their power. There is only one truth, one outcome. The gods have set me on my path, and I will follow it. I must follow it, or...' Layak faltered for a moment.

'Or face your meaninglessness.'

Layak flew at Kulnar, aiming battering overhead blows at his brother. Kulnar deflected each one with apparent ease, swatting the axe-rake left and right, until finally, he swung upwards with the profane blade and knocked the weapon out of Layak's hand. It skidded along snow-covered marble as Layak retreated out of range. He awaited a renewed assault, but Kulnar paused.

'Look upon this city,' the Chaplain said, his voice as the blizzard once more. He was growing in size, taller already than Layak, and still expanding, like some storm giant of ancient mythology. He cast his hands out at the ruined city below, his voice deep and resonating from the stone. 'Every moment of every day, every day since you sent us here, I have studied. There is nothing but knowledge here, but I have found nothing, I have learned *nothing*! There *is* no one truth, Zardu Layak, only a trillion strands of possibilities.'

'Then you have not done enough!' Layak shouted. He raised his left arm, and the ceramite of his armour contorted, peeling back like a flower to reveal the pale skin beneath. Tattoos, brands, and scars twisted on his forearm, different scripts from different civilisations. The subtleties of their meanings changed as the flesh beneath roiled, but they all spoke to one constant: pain.

Pain burned in Layak's nerves as the warp twisted his flesh. He revelled in it. The gods spoke in the language of pain, and they were speaking to *him*, changing *him*. For this moment. He lifted his arm, every part of it screaming in agony – the muscles, skin, sinew, and bone – and spoke a word.

The word coalesced in the air, becoming a shape, sharp as a blade. It hung in the air for a moment, before flying towards Kulnar, hitting him in the chest like a lascannon blast. The impact lifted the Chaplain from the ground, sending him sprawling to the floor, but the shape was not done – it changed form, becoming not a blade but a biting worm, burrowing its way through the ceramite of Kulnar's armour to find the flesh beneath.

It found it, and Kulnar's body shuddered in its supine position as the worm chewed its way into the core of his being. After a long moment, the shuddering stopped. Kulnar sat up, his skin now waxy, his eyes dull, and reached for the Anakatis blade where it had clattered to the floor. He turned the weapon and plunged it through his own chest, his face impassive even as it burst through his armoured back with a gout of blood.

Layak stood over his fallen brother as greasy smoke rose from his corpse. Kulnar's gnarled hand was still curled around the hilt of the Anakatis blade.

'The gods have given me many gifts in your absence,' Layak said. 'Your sorceries are mere tricks compared to the power that I wield now.'

'And yet,' Kulnar said, from behind Layak, 'I remain.'

The corpse was gone, the only reminder a burnt-meat stench in the back of Layak's throat. The Anakatis blade was back in Kulnar's hand, the weapon twitching and fixing its eyes on Layak.

'More tricks.'

'A matter of perspective,' Kulnar said, as he moved past Layak once more to look out across the ruined city. 'From a certain angle, you see the truth.' The shape of the Chaplain burst into snow, falling away with the wind, and a new voice came from Layak's left. Hebek – younger, his face unscarred – stepped forward. 'From another, falsehoods.'

Cursing, Layak beseeched the gods again, speaking words of agony to call forth their power. He raised an arm to channel the black fire, but saw only tattooed script swirl around his wrist. He snarled, and spoke the words again, but felt nothing – no bone-deep pain to signal the arrival of their gifts.

'The gods are fickle with their power,' Kulnar said. 'Capricious entities, they will whisper promises and certainties into the ears of those who will listen. Those who will trust them.'

Layak clenched his fist and roared. Absent the agony of ages past, he channelled his own pain, drawing on the deep wells of the stuff that dwelt within his body. The chastisement at Monarchia. The absence of his primarch. His betrayal of his Emperor. His lies to his Legion. His murder of his brother. Tendrils of black flame licked from his palm, but even as he tried to catch it, to contain it, it guttered and died.

'No,' he whispered, as the pain curled inwards instead, the black fire licking at the core of his being. The question – his question – withered in the flame, and changed its tone.

Why me?

Why me?

Why?

Pain grew to doubt, and doubt burned all it touched. It clawed at certainties, at truths and at beliefs, and left only ash from the great edifice that had been built inside his heart. The ash lifted up and drifted away from a tattooed fist raised to an uncaring galaxy.

'You cannot escape this place,' Kulnar said, as the city disappeared from view. Layak was left alone on the mezzanine, staring out into a void of nothingness. 'But you will find peace here. There are worse fates.'

Shaav stood over the body of Zardu Layak as the Kulnar-phantoms continued their assault, a sea of blood red against the white of the snow. Hebek joined them in their defence of their lord's body, the Anakatis blade carving through multiple Kulnar-ghosts at once. Barnhart's aim was true, and Shaav's psychic pressure kept them from coming too close, but the assault was relentless – as each Kulnar-phantom exploded into snow, another took its place.

Each phantom was the same. No, not quite the same; Layak's memories intermingled with Shaav's own, and Layak had known Kulnar for centuries – he could see the ravages of age in the ghosts' faces. A vision of the Chaplain as a young warrior turned to snow as a las bolt blew through its incorporeal form; a facsimile of Kulnar as Layak's tutor – older, wiser, his face lined by thought – faded just as easily.

Layak's body twitched, and Shaav's concentration faltered, just for a second, as a Kulnar-phantom drew close enough to hit out with its Chaplain's crozius. Shaav caught the blow on his wrist and winced. It was not the full force of an impact from such a weapon – that would have shattered even the arm of his new form – but it was pain nonetheless, the sting of ice on bare skin. He yelped, and projected his aura further, his head throbbing with the effort.

* * *

'Kulnar!' Layak roared, from high in the tower above the void. 'Kulnar!'

He was met only with silence.

'Father...' he said, letting the word escape his lips. The vision of Lorgar was nowhere to be seen.

He was alone.

Despair clawed at his mind, threatening to tear its way in, to flood the void at the core of his being not with purpose, but with doubt.

But it was not the first time he had been alone. Zardu Layak – the boy, the man, the warrior, and the chosen – all stood alone in the face of the galaxy, and all had passed the tests arrayed against them.

In the presence of the gods, no being could be truly alone.

Belief crackled in his chest, and he cast his consciousness far, riding the skeins of reality, searching for a way back.

Far away – so far away – he found a single form, weak and flickering like a candle in a gale. He felt at its edges. It was not his own, but he knew the shape of it. So different, and yet, similar. Lives of loneliness, of misery, of pain. Shared memories, shared experiences, and shared existences connecting the two beings between planes. Their beings converged, and Layak saw through Shaav's eyes once more.

Shaav turned from the blizzard, placing his long-fingered hands on Layak's body, palpating at his torso as if searching for something. With his attention elsewhere, the Kulnar-phantoms came close enough to make out inscriptions on their armour.

'Shaav! What are you doing?' Barnhart yowled.

He heard the question, but offered no answer. He had found what he was looking for. His fingers closed around the hilt of the thin, black-bladed knife.

A Kulnar-ghost breached their defensive line, swinging its fist through the head of one of the Children of the Blessed

Moon – Shaav did not know their name. The impact caved the man's face in, the blood and brain matter freezing before his body hit the ground, before a close-range las bolt turned the phantom into fine mist.

'Shaav, help us! Use your powers!'

She received no response. Shaav stood over the altar, a knife held, point down, over Layak's chest.

'No!' Barnhart screamed, as she leapt forward in a desperate attempt to knock the weapon from his grip.

She was too late. Shaav drove the blade into the Space Marine's chest.

The pain was excruciating, debilitating.

Glorious.

Layak opened his own eyes, and was back in the church, lying across the altar. The blade was still embedded in his chest. He slid it out, feeling hot blood flow into the gash it left in his muscle and organs.

Four figures stood over him. They had been brothers, once, but they were something else now. Subservient to the blade, and the one who wielded it. They stood as if in judgement, but there was to be no justice here.

He tried to move, but the pain was too great. The black blade was not Anakatis, but it was blessed still, imbued by the gods with the power to maximise agony.

Kulnar stood behind his blade slaves. The Chaplain leaned against his Anakatis blade, its tip piercing the snow.

'Greetings, brother,' he said.

Layak grunted, not yet able to marshal a proper response. The pain was lessening, becoming a dull numbness in his extremities.

Someone was still firing their lasgun, the zip and pop of energy impacts muffled, but still audible in the calmed air.

Layak tried to rise, but was forced back to the altar by the closest blade slave.

'I do not blame you, Zardu Layak. You gave me purpose again, for a time. I thought I would find my question here, but you have seen this place. There is no truth to be found.'

Layak wanted to argue, but the void in his gut sucked at his will. Kulnar could read the doubt on his face. He knew him too well.

'No,' he said.

Kulnar turned, scanning the symbols on the wall again. 'We are cousins with the other Legions, but we are so different.'

Layak tried to recite memorised words, but his mind wandered; he tried to draw symbols in the air, but his fingers were sluggish and would not make the necessary shapes.

'It would be a blessing,' Kulnar continued, 'to be a warrior without such a desperate need for purpose – one of Russ' slavering wolves, or Horus' mindless gangers. Even to be one of Guilliman's numberless drones – a simpler existence.' The Chaplain touched his chest. 'Another flaw.' He smiled. 'Our father's original sin.'

Lorgar stood in the snow, as if called into existence by his mentioning. Golden light was reflected in the white, almost blindingly bright. It hurt for Zardu Layak to look at, but he turned his head and opened his eyes, letting the light in, basking in the pain – sharp and hot, vital against the numbness that was taking hold in his body.

'This will hurt,' Kulnar said. 'I am not as cruel as you, brother, but this place needs pain. It needs sacrifice. And I need to keep searching for truth.'

His father found him across the frozen field. The details of Lorgar's face were hidden by the light, but Layak felt him smile. In the wind, a voice. Warm and wise and eternal. The voice of a prophet, of a scholar, of a warrior, and of a father.

'You will suffer what they cannot.'

Agony coursed through Layak's nerves, broken bones trying to knit in a dying body.

'But you will see what they cannot,' four voices said with Lorgar's throat. 'Open your eyes, my child.'

Warmth filled his body, banishing the cold numbness.

Kulnar raised the Anakatis blade over Layak's head. He was speaking, but Layak could no longer hear him.

'I have something you do not,' Layak interrupted.

'What is that?'

'Faith.'

Zardu Layak rose from the altar, using agony as strength. He raised his bleeding hands to his face and felt the heat of his lifeblood against the chill of his skin. His taloned fingers probed at the edges of his eyes, and as they came to rest on the eyeballs themselves, he dug them in, hard. The eyeballs burst, showering aqueous and vitreous humours down his cheeks, and he laughed as he pulled the wreckage of his eyes from their sockets, fleshy strands of nerves, arteries, and veins following them onto the icy floor below.

The world darkened in perfect pain, and he was left with the final image of his own daemonic talons as they pierced the sclera of his eyes. In darkness, his other senses expanded. Layak could taste the familiar copper tang of his own blood in his mouth. He focused on the flavour, hot on his tongue. The wind screamed between ruins he could no longer see, its tone more subtle now he listened for it. It told the tale of this ancient city, of the people who lived here before, of the doom that befell them. He listened to its lament, and he understood their sorrow.

It felt like a lifetime, but in a short moment of unseeing darkness, a light began to shine. Precariously, at first, its brightness guttering like a candle trying to take flame in a draughty temple, but it grew in strength until it banished the black. It illuminated a world around itself – a new world, similar to the one that had stood there before, but so different. A world lit in colours he had never seen, where shadows danced and twirled, where memories and dreams walked the streets – echoes of what had come and what would be.

'Open your eyes,' Lorgar said.

Zardu Layak did as he was asked, and six new eyes opened on his face – flaming orbs sitting in sockets he had clawed in his own flesh.

With his new eyes, he saw what Kulnar could not. The span of time unspooled itself. The ice was replaced by fire, and the city was ruined no more. He stood in the midst of a great conflagration, the moment of doom of this place. The flames should have charred his skin, but he felt nothing – no heat, and no fear. The cataclysm unfolded with all its violence, and he watched it as a scholar, as Kulnar had taught him. He began to notice patterns, persisting in eternal moments: the flame, filling the gaps in the script, over time, revealing the secret of the city, of the people who dwelt within.

There *was* truth here. Its rulers had found it, after millennia of searching – a terrible, universal truth, and when they had found it, they had burned themselves and their city to the ground to protect it from escaping, from being discovered by anyone else.

Layak rose to his feet, pulling the blades from his body as it restored itself in the flames. The numbness had dissipated, replaced by a righteous fire that burned as bright as his new eyes.

Blade slaves lunged for him, but he cast them aside with a burning glance, and closed on Kulnar. The Chaplain shrank as he approached.

'They found the question, Kulnar, and when they asked it, they could not live with the answer.'

Understanding dawned on Kulnar's face. 'I saw the flames, but I thought it was *this* city's end. I was wrong.' He gasped.

Layak saw his six burning eyes reflected in the darkness of Kulnar's pupils. There were tears on the Chaplain's cheeks.

'Ask their question,' Layak commanded.

'How does the galaxy end?' Kulnar asked.

'It ends as it has always ended. As it will always end. It ends with fire. It ends with blood. It ends with Chaos.'

'Wait!' Kulnar shouted. 'What if you are wrong?' It was not a rebuke. There was a pleading in his voice. He wanted to believe, just as Layak did, to allow himself the salve of certainty. 'There is no way back from this.'

Layak laughed, a sound as cold as the wind.

'There is no right or wrong any more, brother, no morality. There is simply truth.' Flames lapped at his ankles as he walked the frozen city, seeing it as it was then, and as it was before. 'Truth is strength, and the gods are strong. They will win, Kulnar. It is inevitable. They are the natural order of our species, the natural order of our galaxy. To fight it – that is the true madness.'

'What if the path you have chosen is the wrong path, the path that dooms us all?'

'I did not choose this path, Kulnar. It was chosen for me. I simply walk it.'

'What happens now?'

'Now I will show you the truth.'

Zardu Layak spoke the words, and the flames consumed him.

Barnhart came back to consciousness slumped against the wall of the church. She remembered only the blade slipping into Layak's chest, before a concussive force had launched her some thirty metres backwards. She was not alone – Ditmar was still out cold, and Palgen was dragging herself to her knees, rubbing the back of her head. The sniper turned to face the altar at the centre of the churchyard, and her face dropped. Barnhart followed her gaze.

A burning giant stood atop the altar, flames rising high from his body.

Shaav wailed – an eerie sound – and fell to his knees in worship.

In ancient times they would have called him an angel. Beautiful and terrible, beyond comprehension in aspect and power. Kulnar shielded his eyes from the creature of flame before him. Six burning eyes bored into his soul regardless, visible through tissue and bone, through time and space.

Kulnar saw what the eyes saw. The city's script, maddeningly beyond understanding before, unfurled in front of him, its meaning finally clear. He read, and saw aeons pass in moments. A million worlds, a trillion souls. All moving – all moved – into place by hands almost invisible, to bring the angel to this place. And he saw the angel himself enter this span, changing – from the man he knew, to the moment that he would become.

The Chaplain saw it then, all of it. A future – *the* future – where Zardu Layak would open the way. From a world of fire to a galaxy aflame, Kulnar saw not an infinity of futures, but one future – one path.

'Too human,' Layak said, his voice like solar wind. 'Doubt is a weakness of the species. But fear not, brother, I will show them the truth behind the cosmos. I will show them the face of the gods.' Where he stepped, the ice melted, and the city burned.

Kulnar cowered as the angel stood over him.

'You are chosen…' Kulnar repeated. It could not be denied, not any longer. 'I know.' He licked parched lips, and tasted ash. 'I have always known. It was written in your future. I could not accept the truth.' Kulnar touched his chest a final time. 'Another flaw,' he said.

Kulnar raised the Anakatis blade to his own neck. It thrummed in his hand

'Goodbye, brother,' he said.

Kulnar slid the ragged edge of the Anakatis blade across his throat, deep enough that he felt the edge bite into the bone of his spine. The weapon squealed as it drank his hot blood, and he slumped to the snow. He felt the cold as the colour faded from his vision, the pristine white turning blood red, before fading to ash black.

Kulnar stepped into the circle.

'Have you made your selection?' Ko-Farak asked.

'I have,' Kulnar said.

'Speak the name, so that we may stand in judgement.'

He spoke Zardu Layak's Legion name.

'The boy?' Saucan asked, with a sneer in his voice. 'The Chapter of the Ochre Gate can field some of the finest warriors in the Legion. Why him?'

Because he is fated, Kulnar thought, turning to face Saucan. Because his rise is foretold. This is the next step on his path, and I have no choice but to put him on it.

The Chaplain had consulted books – so many books – of scripture and verse, of prophecy and of science. He had been looking for an answer, the answer to the question he had always asked. But he found something else across their pages and diagrams.

He had found a thread. It was a fine thread, so fine as to be almost invisible, and at first he took it for a trick of the light. A coincidence, writings and ravings from the mad and sane across the galaxy pointing him in one direction. But no matter how often he tried to explain it away with logic and reason, the thread remained, catching the light.

So he started to pull on the thread. He was a scholar, he told himself. Despite his doubt, he had to see where it went.

It had led him here. To stand in front of his brothers, his squad-mates, in a circle of purity. And now he would lie. To them, and to himself.

PART THREE

FIDELITAS

CHAPTER SEVEN

The axe-rakes collided with a ring like a prayer bell. It echoed through the practice cages, serving to call those Word Bearers of the Chapter of the Ochre Gate not currently involved in their own training bouts to watch their Chapter Master spar with their newest sergeant.

The weapons' chainblades were deactivated – Saucan's one concession to the fight as a training exercise – but they still delivered blows that could cleave ceramite and break bone. The man who would become Zardu Layak's armour bore the scars to prove it.

'A challenge!' Saucan roared, as he batted aside Layak's swing. The force of the impact almost took the weapon from Layak's hand. 'Make it a challenge, boy! You are too predictable!' Saucan twisted his wrist with the parry, and spun, adding momentum to a strike that, had Layak not half-caught his Chapter Master's arm, would have removed the top of his skull. Layak wrapped his fingers around Saucan's wrist, and tried to pull him forward, but the Chapter Master was bigger, and pulled him forwards instead. Layak didn't try to fight the balance shift, rolling with it instead, bringing his

axe-rake forward for a thrusting strike designed to catch Saucan in the groin.

There was a wumph *and a blast of superheated air as the Chapter Master launched backwards, out of the range of the weapon. He came to rest a few metres away, his jump pack whining as its engines cycled back down.*

'Better!' Saucan called, as he paced, keeping his distance from the younger Space Marine. 'But you rely too much on your blade. A true warrior uses every weapon at his disposal.'

The Chapter Master raised his hand flamer, pointing the wrist-mounted weapon at Layak. Layak's own flamer had been disabled prior to the training session, as was procedure in the practice cages.

'I hope that you will learn from this,' Saucan said, as a gout of flame roared from his weapon. 'No fight is truly fair.'

Saucan had retired to his chambers after his time in the practice cages. Other challengers had come after Layak, but still he relived the bout.

A chime split his focus, and he turned to the source of it. A green light flashed above a button, insistent. He reached for the button, and paused, taking a second to compose himself before tapping it.

A mellifluous voice filled his chamber as the contact spoke.

'Report the boy's progress.'

'Physically, he has reacted well to his elevation. His body is strong, he is fast, and he handles bolter and blade as well as any in his cohort.'

'Good,' *the contact said.* 'Very good.'

'But the other tests...'

'Yes?' *the contact said. Even through the creature, Saucan could sense annoyance.*

'The boy has shown some psychic aptitude. He might be a candidate for the Librarius. For the Chapter of the Void. He may serve better there, in supervised conditions.'

'No,' *his contact said.* 'He will join you. He will join the Chapter of the Ochre Gate.'

'My lord, his mind is... damaged. He was a poor specimen when he was discovered. His markers would have seen him eliminated on sight, but for some reason, this did not take place. I have already reprimanded the brother responsible for sparing his life. He should not have reached aspirant status, let alone made the ranks of the Legion.'

'And yet he did.'

'A mistake.'

A moment of silence passed, and Saucan knew he had overstepped. A hiss came over the channel, and he hoped it was signal interference.

'Be careful, Chapter Master,' *the contact said.* 'Your elevation was swift. Your fall may be similarly sudden.'

Saucan took a breath, and worked to keep his tone neutral. 'Yes, my lord,' he said. 'I did not–'

'You may think me far away, child, but I promise you...' The whisper came from Saucan's left shoulder, a voice in the room as real as his own. 'I am always watching.'

Layak prayed in the church for a time. He allowed the flames to touch his skin, their blessed pain bringing certainty. Kulnar's own blade slaves had died as soon as the Anakatis touched their master's throat – their bodies were crackling softly in the churchyard, skin and armour blackened. Only Kulnar and Hebek stood alongside their brother, silent and still in the eye of the firestorm that was consuming what remained of the city.

He could see his brothers more perfectly than ever before. His new eyes saw beyond their physical frames, to the men they had been. Their triumphs and their tragedies, their memories of lives lived as humanity's greatest weapons – all were laid bare to the man who was their master.

Hebek's path was simple, but while Kulnar's mind was open,

his memories were a tangled web. Half-formed theories and understandings clouded his mind, as incomplete as the script that adorned the frozen city's walls had been.

Pain, as always, brought clarity. Layak spoke words of flesh-craft, twisting Kulnar's body, wrenching bone and searing nerves.

The warrior did not cry out – did not even twitch – but the memories in his mind sharpened, like a hololithic projector being tuned. Layak saw the strongest memories as bright points seared into the grey matter of Kulnar's brain: his rise to Legion brother, his promotion to Chaplain, even his exile to this world. Between them, smaller memories, outlined in pain. He had not been able to decipher the frozen city's final question, but he had learned much from the place – psychic methods and sorceries developed by a people that had devoted their whole civilisation to the Anakatis.

The Anakatis. Layak seized on the memory, and followed the thread backwards, tracing its blade edge through Kulnar's mind to the source.

He found it. A mountain, dark as night even as it rose against the white sky. It had been the blades' resting place on this world, before settlers had come and taken them, splitting the three from each other. Only one remained in its grave, deep below the mountain – the most powerful of its kin.

Hebek and Kulnar had claimed their prizes and made their monuments far from the mountain, where they were free to exert their control, or seek the understanding they craved. But Saucan – always the most fiery of temperament – had stayed where the Anakatis had lain.

The mountain was far from here, in Helwain's southern hemisphere. Layak could see the path – a bright line, leading across deserts and oceans, valleys and tundra, leading him to his end, and a new beginning.

* * *

They had arrived in five landers, a force almost five hundred strong. So many men and women – and in Jassim's case, something else entirely – had found their graves on this world.

Only eight remained. They filed from the burning city like insects, tiny black specks against the snowplain, running to their salvation with as much energy as remained to them. Barnhart watched them arrive at the landing point, bloodied and in many cases broken by their ordeal. Blood oozed from Ditmar's temple, and – from the way his eyes swivelled in his head – Barnhart wagered his skull was fractured in more than one place. Palgen spoke to herself in whispered tones, reliving the battle, recounting the impossibilities she had seen. Fingernails traced the same symbol over and over in the skin of her forehead, Barnhart noticed. Blood was starting to seep from the scratches.

She had waited as long as she could in the church, but the flames had beaten the Children of the Blessed Moon back. Bereft, broken, and with Layak unresponsive to vox-transmissions, they had retreated to the lander.

No more of her Children came from the city. No more would, she knew. What remained of their bodies would be ash, to be carried away by the winds. She climbed the lander's boarding ramp, pulling the handle that closed the door as she made her way through the boxy craft.

She slid into the cockpit's low-slung seat. An array of brightly coloured buttons lay in front of her. She took the flight stick in her hand, but could barely feel its curved grip beneath her thick gloves.

For a blessed moment, Barnhart considered her options in silence. They could make their way to the deserted capital, find a communications array. A distress signal might reach a vessel in the area, might pull them down to this forgotten world. They could survive all this. They could be rescued.

And then what? They would be picked up by forces loyal to the Emperor, who would execute them on sight for their treason. More likely they would be rescued by Word Bearers vessels following *The Path Less Travelled*'s warp signature, and put back into service for the Legion as fodder troops, punished for their failure. Or they would simply die in the abandoned city, victims of starvation, predation, or simple madness, the strains on their psyches too great.

She wasn't sure which option was worse.

The chime of her vox-unit brought her from her reverie. She knew who would speak before she thumbed the receiver.

'Lieutenant,' Layak said. The vox-transmission was underscored with a strange hiss – a sound she had not heard on the unit before. *'Our paths are destined to cross again.'*

No peace, she thought. Not for us.

Flipping switches, she took the flight stick in steady hands. 'Hang on,' Barnhart said over the internal vox, as she ignited the lander's engines. 'We're going to pick up some passengers.'

The Space Marine had given her a loose location, but it was not necessary. Barnhart knew where Layak would be, knew that the Space Marine was still alive. She couldn't explain her certainty. Perhaps it was intuition, or battlefield sense, or…

Fate.

The voice that spoke the words was her own. Unbidden, it had come to her mind, a sudden spike of clarity that she could not shake.

'Lieutenant? Is everything all right?' Ditmar asked over the vox, and Barnhart realised she had broadcast her vocalisation to her soldiers.

'Nothing. Vox-interference,' she replied, cutting the link.

Fate?

Barnhart did not believe in fate – she had seen too much

randomness in the galaxy. The same could not be said for many of her soldiers. Since their assignment to the Word Bearers, the men and women of the unit had been changing. Pamphlets and palimpsests had been passed between the troops, secretly at first, between the lower ranks, but then more openly. She had read them, of course, skimming the proclamations of doom and the declarations of divinity. Such things were not new to her as they were the younger soldiers, and held less sway. She knew the pull of fervour, of zealotry. It was the reason she was here at all – the thrill of belief was what had dragged her from her comfortable existence, and she could not forgive it for that.

But Barnhart was a pragmatic soldier, and she navigated the blossoming of faith in these new gods carefully. Her circumspection – combined with her sound judgement – had allowed her to rise steadily through the ranks of the Children of the Blessed Moon. She did not baulk when the unit shed its long history as the Koifaul 117th and found its new name – a name taken from prophecy, as backward as the custom seemed. Belief had always been a seed in the unit, but it was cultivated by life among the Word Bearers.

Whether there were gods or not, it had not mattered to Yergorin Barnhart. All that had mattered was her survival, the survival of the men and women under her command.

And yet.

She saw Layak before the lander's auspex scanner identified his armour's signal. He walked a path through the twice-destroyed city, narrow, but somehow clear of the rubble and rock that covered the ground. Two figures followed him, both dragging enormous blades that carved furrows in the ash and snow. She would deliver Layak to his goal, just as he would deliver…

Fate.

Barnhart kicked the lander into a sharp turn, dialling back power to the engines as she came to hover a few inches above the charred earth. She pulled the hatch release in the cockpit and shuddered as she heard heavy boots hit the access ramp.

The mountain rose from a forest in the planet's southern hemisphere. It was nondescript, one of a small range, not the tallest of its siblings nor the smallest. It was roughly conical in shape, its sides somewhere between shallow and steep, and had no caldera to indicate any volcanic activity, either ancient or recent. It was, empirically, like a thousand other mountains on Helwain.

But it was different. Beneath the mountain was where Layak would find Saucan, and the final Anakatis blade.

'Prepare for landing in sixty seconds,' Barnhart called, as the lander dipped in the sky. The mountain grew larger in the viewport, already a vast edifice of stone, blocking the light of the weak sun.

Layak breathed slowly, tasting the recycled air of the vessel. He felt Kulnar and Hebek at his left and right shoulders, felt their impossible stillness. He tried to close his eyes, to meditate in their exquisite agony, but he found his new eyes could not close. Even when he tried, he could still see the faces of the remaining human passengers, eyes wide and teeth grinding as they stared at the giants in their midst.

'Do we scare you?' he asked the closest man, who involuntarily threw himself sideways in his seat at the sound of Layak's voice, booming inside the lander. Saved only from the indignity of falling onto the floor by his crash webbing, the man recovered, and stuttered a reply.

'No, my lord! It is the greatest honour of my life to serve alongside you and your brothers.'

'You lie,' Layak said, smiling. Fear radiated from the man like smoke. Dark tendrils of it coiled from the mortal's mouth and wrapped themselves around his throat, terror made manifest to Layak's new sight. Layak thanked the gods again for their gift, and let the man struggle as words caught in his throat, before he spoke again. 'Do not worry,' he said, leaning close to the man, until he could smell his sour breath. 'So do I.'

'Touchdown in five, four, three, two, one.'

A jolt, and then the sound of the engines whining as they cycled down. Layak rose, and took the next step along his path.

CHAPTER EIGHT

On closer inspection, the mountain was not so much like its peers. Where they had been created by tectonic violence, their spires built from pressurised or superheated rock, it had been formed from layers of sediment. The geology gave the mountain a peculiar yellow-brown colour, visible only as Layak's boots scraped through the top layer of dark earth that lay around its lower reaches.

There were signs of habitation, too, or at least some form of civilisation. Paths had been worn into the rock, around which the scrubby forest trees had not encroached, ways that members of fallen civilisations had followed on their pilgrimages. The mountain was a place of worship; Layak could feel the residue of the stuff in the sandy stone. With his new gifts, he could see it – ancient devotion shimmering from the rock like heat haze on a hot afternoon.

They walked the path. Yergorin Barnhart and no more than seven of her soldiers, their cold weather gear thrown off in the temperate climate, exposing ripped and bloodstained undersuits. Shaav padded alongside them, a stalking beast, his form phasing in and out of corporeality. Bringing up the rear, Layak's blade slaves – dead brothers now trusted to carry the weapons that they had given themselves to. He led what remained of his force onwards on the path, towards the heart of the mountain.

The path led to a cave, and just like the trail, it was not of natural construction – sentient hands had scraped away at the soft rock with simple tools, creating a route into the depths of the mountain, descending. The sun had returned to Helwain's sky, but Yergorin Barnhart could see only blackness beyond the cave's entrance. She paused at the threshold, and her soldiers, noticing her reticence, stopped alongside her. All were beyond the hand signals of their training now – they were operating on animal instinct alone.

A voice came from behind her, surprising in its softness.

'You are afraid,' Zardu Layak said.

It was not a question this time. Barnhart turned, meeting the eyes of her remaining soldiers. She saw the wild glint of madness in some, their minds pushed too far. In others, just the dull thrum of exhaustion, bone-deep. In all, though, she saw fear. Trapped animals, all who remained, hamstrung by duty and circumstance, unable to escape their end.

'Yes, my lord,' Barnhart said. 'We all are.'

'What do you fear you will find inside?' Once again, there was no judgement in his tone, just a disarming curiosity.

'Death, my lord.'

'There are worse things than death, lieutenant.'

'I know. I have seen them. But it is not simply death I fear. I have seen a thousand deaths, my lord, of all kinds – good and bad. I have seen friends become vapour in the space of an eyeblink. I have seen enemies torn apart, their heads still screaming as they are removed from their bodies. This very day I have seen death, and have delivered my own mercy to souls who did and did not deserve it.'

The words unspooled, and she expected a rebuke for speaking so frankly. But Layak listened to every word, as still as his silent companions.

'I made the choice to leave my home, to join the military, and now I find myself involved in a galactic civil war, and... more, beyond which I could ever explain. I have to believe that choice to leave was my own, or the reality of my existence would destroy me.'

She felt the void of the cave behind her. A black hole, its gravity pulling her in. The terrible inevitability of it all.

'I believed in something, once. I thought I did. But then I saw the violence of the galaxy, the callousness, and how could I believe that there was a purpose to it all? I could only believe in myself. That my life was my own.' She swallowed the lump in her throat. 'I wish only for my death to be the same. I fear that it will not be.'

Layak stared at her, a statue carved in grey stone. She waited for castigation.

'I understand,' he said, finally.

'You do?' she asked, surprised.

'More than you know,' Layak said. 'You speak of destiny. I know it well. But there is always a choice, lieutenant.'

'What is that?'

'How you meet your fate. Run from it, and it will find you, weak and broken. I choose to embrace it.'

Layak reached up, and slid his helmet from his head. He raised his face to the sun, and for the first time, she saw his new face. Six eyes burned like hot coals in his pale skin, three in two rows on either side of a fanged maw. A forked tongue lay beyond the teeth, its movements spilling black bile across cracked lips. Tattoos and brands covered his head from front to back, runes and symbols describing blasphemies and atrocities, permanent markings in honour of the Ruinous Powers.

He was a creature of nightmares, a vision of humanity's oldest fears brought to life, and yet she did not scream. She did not startle.

She looked upon the monster, and she was not afraid.

In those burning eyes, she saw her own flame, reflected. The same fire that burned in her heart on the day she left Koifaul, the fire that drove her forward when all seemed lost. It had burned her, that fire, and she could only salve those wounds by making herself cold. But the fire still burned inside her – she still had belief.

She looked into his eyes, and knew that Layak had a purpose.

She had a purpose.

'You are here, with me, in this place,' Layak said. 'Because you are meant to be.' He stepped forward, and held out a hand, guiding her into the mountain, further along the path.

'Be not afraid, child. We are chosen.'

The bones appeared long before they reached the final chamber, as Barnhart and her remaining troops marched through the wide tunnels. Just a few at first. Knuckles and fingers, others small enough that she had taken them as rocks, and crushed them under her boots. But these smaller bones were soon joined by bigger ones: femurs and ulnas, ribs and hips. Skulls, soon after, some toothless with age, others still covered with patches of leathery skin, still bearing tufts of wiry hair. Protected from the sun, in the muggy environment of the mountain, they had not decomposed as bodies would have done on the surface.

Not human, she told herself. Their bones were too strange to be human, their jaws too long, their eye sockets too large, their hands gnarled into claws. And yet, they had the shape of humanity: two arms, two legs, their skulls bearing much the same mirthless grin as her own would, long after her demise.

She had avoided them at first, stepping carefully over each bone, around each skin-wrapped bundle, but as they descended further, they became so frequent that she could not chart a course without kicking them aside or smashing them to dust. Even as someone so familiar with death, she had never seen so many bodies.

The red glow faltered as Ditmar slumped to the ground, dropping the flare he was carrying. Barnhart turned, and tried to help the soldier to his feet, but his arm was slack, his body a dead weight. She knelt next to him, and turned him over, supporting his head with her arm as she pried open a half-closed eye with her fingers. His pupils were huge, black holes into a mind that was losing its consciousness. It would soon be gone for good. Liquid ran down his cheeks, a darker river of something slick. Blood or tears. In the red flare light, she couldn't tell.

'Rest easy,' she said, still supporting his head. At the sound of her voice, his eyes refocused slightly, and a smile of recognition crossed his stained face.

'Mother?' he asked.

She had no children, and yet she answered.

'Yes, my child?'

'Did we do the right thing?'

She paused. A flicker of confusion danced on his features, and he looked so very young for a moment. A spear of pity lanced her heart, and she comforted him. 'I believe we did. We are here for a reason. You are here for a reason.' She wiped liquid from his cheek with her thumb, and touched her forefinger to the centre of his head. 'The Blessed Moon watches over you, child. Even here.'

Ditmar looked up, towards the rock ceiling above, and smiled as his eyes lost their focus.

'The gods…' he breathed. 'I can see them. They're watching us.'

Barnhart followed his gaze and, impossibly, saw the moon, twinkling among stars, like eyes in the dark.

Ditmar drew a final breath, pulling her focus back to his face, where the last light in his eyes died. Barnhart laid his head down as gently as she could, nestled amongst the bodies of long-dead beings. She heaved her lasgun over her shoulder, and stood.

Layak had stopped and was watching her, his two silent companions at his shoulders. She spared a glance upwards again, but could see only red-bathed rock. She called her remaining soldiers onwards.

The gate rose before them at the end of the path, barring the way into the mountain. It was a simple structure – carved of stone, and decorated with primordial symbols, it had nonetheless resisted any attempts to breach it, be they sorcerous or more mechanical. Scorch marks darkened the rock at the base of the gate where those attempts had failed.

Zardu Layak was pacing in front of the gate, a predator unable to reach its prey. The gate kept him from Saucan, and his final test. Shaav stood as far away as possible while still keeping his eyes on the Space Marine, watching as he paused his pacing to scrawl symbols on the stone wall. Shaav found he recognised the symbols as invocations of the Dark Gods – the time Layak had spent in his bodies leaving an imprint of his being.

He tried to focus on them, to take his attention from the sound at the back of his mind. At first, when they had entered the mountain, he had thought the sound was a simple echo, his own whispered affirmation reflected back from the red-lit stone walls. But as they had descended further into the mountain's heart, as the thick heat rose and the skeletal bodies began to form piles, he had halted his own whispering, yet the echo remained, clawing at the back of his thoughts, like the wind through empty streets.

Don't, he thought, but it was too late. Involuntarily, he had tuned his senses to the echo, and he realised with a terrible, yawning horror that it was not an echo at all, but words.

They were formed of sounds that he had never heard, made with symbols that he had never drawn, but he could understand them. They were born from alphabets beyond his knowledge, in languages beyond human capabilities, and still he could understand them.

He could understand them, because he had seen them before, had studied them before, through eyes that were not his own. He knew where they lay, each hieroglyph and rune, each symbol and each word – among a great collection, drawn together by a beast that presided over its secret hoard. Layak's memories had taken root in his own mind, inscribing it with new memories, new knowledge, just as his body had been changed.

A lifetime stretched out behind him, a life longer than he could imagine, filled with more pain than he thought possible. It rose like a sun in the sky, a blinding light that eclipsed his own pain.

His own memories.

His own being.

'No, no,' he whimpered. 'I am Dasich Shaav, I am Dasich Shaav, I am–'

'You are not,' Lorgar said. 'Not any more.'

Shaav had never seen a being so beautiful. Bathed in golden light, Shaav would have thought him an angel, but Layak's memories were supplanting his own, and he knew the angel as his father instead.

'I am... What am I?' he asked, his drooping lips struggling to make the words.

'You are empty. You are nothing.'

'I can't remember...'

'You are a vessel.'

'What... what am I for?'

'For this moment.'

Lorgar stopped and faced Shaav.

The meaning of the words hit Shaav like a krak grenade, and he stumbled and fell, his changed body already unstable on rearranged legs. Nobody helped him to his feet.

'Please, no...'

'You are fated, Shaav. You have a part to play as well. The gods see all – even their lowliest souls.'

Shaav looked to Layak. The Space Marine had stopped pacing and was watching him, his burning eyes bright.

'The mountain demands the final sacrifice,' Layak explained, understanding it as Shaav did, their two souls connected. 'The death of those who wish to enter.'

Layak raised his hand, and Shaav was beside him, his powers pulling him closer with a word.

'I see it now,' Layak said.

The sorcery had been perfected by the kings of the frozen city, a method of transferring their being – and its accumulated knowledge – through generations. Kulnar had studied it during his years of exile, and so Layak knew it too. He knew the cost.

The grey armour across Layak's chest was blackening with clotting blood, as gifts both biological and gods-given helped to seal the wound Shaav had opened with the black dagger. Layak split it open once more, reaching his hand into the gouge in his armour, pushing aside sinew and rib, searching for something deep inside himself. Blood spurted from the hole in his chest, running the length of his bare wrist, and agony took him from his feet. He fell to his knees, his own hand still inside his body, until he found what he had been searching for.

Zardu Layak pulled a ball of shimmering darkness from inside his body. Gore painted the stone floor of the chamber as he cradled the ball, gasping as his ribcage once more began the painful process of knitting itself back together.

The ball quivered like a frightened animal, its blackness swirling and shifting. Layak closed his hand around it, marshalling the strength to stand.

He laid a gauntleted hand on Shaav's shoulder, steadying himself as he drew to his feet. The misshapen creature quaked at his touch, despite its gentleness.

He dared look into Layak's face, and saw his six blazing eyes were weeping blood.

Layak's bare fist punched up through Shaav's abdomen, destroying inhuman flesh, until it reached his chest. Shaav's eyes widened, the movement so quick he could not yet feel the pain, and Layak released the shimmering ball inside his body.

Numbness swept over Shaav, and his vision narrowed. The chamber and the gate suddenly seemed very far away, as his consciousness lost its grip on his body. He saw himself as if from above, slipping away from his malformed shape, out into the darkened sea beyond.

He was a ghost again, once more haunting this world – but this time, he would not find his way back.

When Zardu Layak slid his fist out from the creature's stomach, it was not Dasich Shaav any more. It was a vessel for Layak's memories. Memories of fear and shame, mercy and doubt. The very memories that had made him human.

It was the lonely child on the orbital, weeping amongst treasures from a world he had never seen. It was the liar and the betrayer, shame sickening his soul. It was the believer, kneeling amongst the ruins of Monarchia, castigated by the being he was born to worship.

Black fluid still oozing from the hole in his stomach, Layak pulled the creature from its feet, lifting the thing that had been Dasich Shaav like a sacrificial animal. He bared Shaav's long neck, and cut his throat with the black knife, killing his memories in a single stroke. Blood cascaded from the gash, thick and pungent, coating the stone. It rumbled open, as a lifetime of misery and suffering bled out onto the cavern floor.

CHAPTER NINE

Heat hit Barnhart like a backhand to the face, a wall of sick-smelling warmth that made her retch. She spat the foulness from her mouth, steeled herself, and stepped through the gate.

The entrance chamber had been expansive, but the space beyond was an order of magnitude larger. The mountain had been hollowed out, and they had come in roughly halfway up its side, finding themselves on a walkway created from the bones of a long-dead beast. In life, it must have been a horrifying sight – an unfathomably huge serpent, it had wormed its way through the layers of rock as if it was water. Petrified ribs and vertebrae jutted from above and below, acting almost as structural supports for the hollow mountain. Perhaps the creature itself had carved out this domain, curling around the blades it protected. Or perhaps, it – like her – was not of this place, but had been trapped here, destined to end its unimaginable life at the point of the cursed weapons.

The bone walkway led downwards to the cavern floor far

below. That floor was broken by vast pits of bubbling liquid, lit from within by an unearthly glow. Barnhart could not tell what the liquid was, but as she watched, she saw figures haul themselves out of the pits, their movements awkward and off balance. Rising above the pits, in the centre of the chamber, stood a stone dais.

Above, the glow gave way to a darkness that obscured the distant rock ceiling. The silhouettes of gliding creatures were briefly visible as they flitted between tall outcroppings of rock far overhead, their shapes almost human, but for the wings that stretched from their shoulders.

'What is this place?' Palgen breathed.

'I don't know,' Barnhart said, as she stared across the cavern and felt her skin crawl. The figures below had halted their work and were now looking up at the interlopers, limbs raised to point in anger. A ululating roar came from the floor of the chamber, and the figures moved as one, making for the base of the ramp. Layak snarled in response and pitched forward into a run, joined a moment later by his silent companions, dragging their awful blades behind them.

The Children of the Blessed Moon looked to her.

'Weapons ready!' Barnhart called, snapping them from their inaction. 'Select priority targets, and keep moving. And may the gods forever watch over you.'

Her own hands were slick with sweat as she brought her weapon round. It was the heat, she told herself, as she checked her lasgun's power pack, pulled its stock into her shoulder, and set off after Zardu Layak.

From a distance, she could see that the things below were big – their bodies were corded with muscle, their wide shoulders covered in ragged scraps of clothing. But as she reached the floor of the chamber, she saw that they were horribly different.

The base shape was human, with recognisable shapes of arms

and legs, heads and shoulders. But they were humans as imagined through a broken lens. No two were alike. Some moved like animals, propelling themselves on hyper-muscled arms or leaping forward like bloodsucking insects on knees that bent in reverse. Others were stranger still. Barnhart watched as the stomach of one mutant opened to reveal a row of teeth, glistening with ichor as a long tongue played along their sharpened edges. Their skin had a pulpy effect to it, still rippling in places, as if infested by vermin, or like half-cooked dough attempting to rise.

Already, Layak was moving through them, cutting them down with an unnerving ferocity. He used his axe-rake sparingly, pulling their bodies apart instead with a gesture, or launching cascades of flame or flickering lightning from his fingertips. When he did use his axe-rake, it was with righteous anger – the weapon rising high, as though he were a priest calling a sermon, before being brought down on the skulls and necks of the heathens below. His silent companions were his acolytes, their massive blades clearing the path before their master, and delivering mercy to any half-dead stragglers left in his wake.

Barnhart and her remaining troops tried to follow the procession, keeping a loose circle. A squat mutant, wider than it was tall, its neck subsumed into its muscled torso, elbowed its cousins out of the way as it barrelled towards Barnhart. Her first las bolt caught it in the shoulder, and it flinched – not enough to alter its course. She squeezed the trigger again, aiming for the knee this time as she backed away from the beast. The bolt missed, and she cursed. The memory called something else back from her childhood, and as she brought the lasgun's ironsight to her eye, she did something she had not done for half a lifetime.

She prayed.

'Gods,' she said. 'Help my aim be true.'

The shot clipped the mutant in the shin, and it fell hard, its massive upper body slamming into the rock. It tried to lift its head, and she saw its expression of anger become one of confusion as the Anakatis blade sliced through it from behind, bisecting it completely in a diagonal cut from shoulder to waist. Layak's silent companion was already moving for another target as the upper half of the mutant slid slowly to the floor, its blood turning the stone the same crimson red as the Space Marine's armour.

They were Zardu Layak's brothers. Some connection – in bone, or blood, or whatever remained of a soul – told him that truth. That the things that hauled themselves out of the flesh pits, that crawled and galloped to stop him reaching his prize, were creatures born of Space Marine gene-seed.

His axe-rake swung into the ribcage of one mutant, mulching skin and muscle, and catching against the reinforced bone beneath. Layak pulled the thing closer with the weapon, staring into its eyes. Gold flecks shone in their depths, just the tiniest remnant of their gene-father. A dignity denied them. Bastard sons of Lorgar, born in the dark to die, never to meet their primarch, never to know of the gods.

Flickers of pity rose in his stomach. The sensation was almost alien to him now, and he observed it rather than felt it, cataloguing it as an artefact of a past life. The gods did not pity, so he did not pity.

The perfect vessel.

'You are delivered,' Layak whispered into the mutant's face, as he punched his bladed fist into its stomach. The mutant did not scream – did not even make a sound – watching in mute acceptance as Layak blasted open its ribcage, and its innards spilled to the dusty floor. He put a boot into its chest, simultaneously kicking it backwards and wrenching his arm from the corpse, splattering his grey armour with red blood.

The altar stood above, on the central dais. The final Anakatis blade was atop it, the only one of its siblings to remain in its resting place. Saucan would be close by – he was no indolent king, and would not stand by while there was fighting to be done.

A detonation on the ceramite of his left shoulder pauldron spun Layak around, pulling him from his thoughts.

One step along the path at a time, he reminded himself, as a second explosion kicked up splintered stone at his feet. Using the forms of Hebek and Kulnar as cover, he scanned the battlefield for the source of the explosions. He found it soon enough.

It was a blasphemy. It moved towards him, taller even than its malformed peers, clad in red Mark III power armour, its surface inscribed with crude copies of the markings and symbols of his own Chapter. Colchisian runes and esoteric symbols had been rendered meaningless in their replication, like a child trying to play at something it did not yet understand. Its bare head was shaven, its ochre-brown skin shining in the glow. Compared to its malformed brothers, this one was a success, standing as tall as Layak did on strong legs, its arms cradling a battered and scratched Umbra-pattern bolter. It fired the weapon again as it stepped forward, forcing Layak to duck behind Hebek. The blade slave quivered as the bolter shells blossomed against his body, gouging pits in the ceramite of his armour, and blasting away gobbets of the meat beneath. His flesh writhed in response, skin, teeth, hair, and muscle working to close the wounds, the Anakatis blade rebuilding the body in its own image.

Layak fired his bolt pistol back, but the armoured mutant was fast, and the bolt shells sailed past, detonating amongst less fortunate mutants behind. Layak moved to chase, but fleshy pincers grabbed at his leg. He stamped without looking down, feeling the crunch of skull under boot, hearing the splatter of exploded brain on ceramite.

Another bolt shell caromed off his vambrace, the impact knocking the bolt pistol from his hand, sending it skidding into the flesh pits. Three more red-armoured warriors stood at the edge of the dais, tall and strong, bolters raised, their muzzles smoking. Their bare heads were unadorned with tattoos or brands, their eyes flecked with gold – perfect copies of each other. Perfect copies of Saucan.

The Chapter Master stood behind his creations. He wore a robe of skin, stretched over armour the stone grey of the Legion's past. It was decorated not with the symbology of the Ruinous Powers, as had increasingly become custom, but in the older style, with commemorations of the Legion's triumphs. Parchment hung from wax seals, dedications to the campaigns of Corrinos and Holger, phylacteries and reliquaries containing remnants of burned worlds dangling from his pauldrons and back-mounted power pack. The grandest memento had pride of place in the centre of his breastplate, above his hearts: a gilded skull, the Colchisian runes for 'Monarchia' inscribed across its forehead.

'Welcome, brother,' Saucan called. His voice filled the vast space, resonant and deep, and across the chamber the mutants turned to regard him, bowing their heads in supplication. Hebek and Kulnar stopped, too, their Anakatis blades falling loose in their hands. They turned to look at their Chapter Master, compelled either by memory, or by the call of the final blade over its siblings.

'You have changed much since we last met,' Saucan said, as Layak fixed burning eyes upon him. The Chapter Master reached up, and slipped his ornate helm from his head. Stubby protrusions of bone rose from his hairless scalp, the skin red and angry where they had burst through. His eyes, once gold-flecked in the image of his primarch, were now a pale green. 'But then, so have I.'

Layak flicked gore from his axe-rake, and spoke.

'The blade is mine.'

'This blade?' Saucan asked. He stepped to the centre of the dais, and closed his hand around the final Anakatis blade, lifting it from the altar on which it lay. Two indentations lay empty next to it, the resting places for the other two blades. He brought the weapon close to his face, allowing the eyes that studded its surface to take him in. A protuberance of flesh and vertebrae twisted from its hilt, palpating at Saucan's gauntlets until it coiled itself around his wrist with a contented sigh, securing itself to its wielder.

'On the contrary,' Saucan said, his voice rimed with contempt. 'It is mine.' He swung the weapon in a lazy arc, turning back to face Layak below. 'But you never did have a true grasp of loyalty.'

'This is no loyalty,' Layak said, gesturing at the mutants that filled the chamber. 'You preside over a kingdom of monsters, a mockery of our Legion.'

'They are the future of our Legion,' Saucan roared. 'They are your brothers, just as strong as any in the Chapter – I have made sure of it.' He stood behind the armoured warriors, inspecting them as if on the parade ground.

'We should have known the Emperor was no god. Gods are not fallible, and yet he failed us, brother.' Saucan banged the hilt of the Anakatis blade against his breastplate, striking the gilded skull embedded there. 'He bred us with no fear, but he left our fickleness, our ambition, our pride.'

He held the Anakatis blade high, a symbol in the gloom.

'I have removed these sins. My warriors know only obedience. They know only power, and they are loyal to that power. It is a wonderful thing, this blade. It ensures that they will fight at my side as we take the galaxy once more.'

'You cannot take a galaxy hiding under a mountain,' Layak said.

Saucan's green eyes flashed. 'I will not dwell here forever. I am marshalling my forces to rebuild our Legion. Think of the glorious conquest that would once again take to the stars. Not in the name of the false Emperor, but in the name of the Bearers of the Word. We will spread enlightenment once more, and throw off the yoke of tyranny.'

'And for you?'

'A legacy. Reward for my own efforts, my own loyalty. I will be known as the saviour of the Seventeenth. To bring us from our shame, to our glory. To right the wrongs performed against us, to grind Guilliman and his Legion under the wheel of history.'

Saucan stepped to the edge of the dais, above Layak. The mutants shuffled backwards, genuflecting to the blade and its wielder.

'You could still join us, boy.'

'That future will not come to pass,' Layak said.

'How can you be so sure?'

'Because I have seen it. The future is foretold, Saucan. All we can do is play our parts.'

Saucan's smile widened. 'And if I reject your future?'

'Then you will be destroyed.'

Saucan smiled. A cruel smile. 'I rather hoped you would say that.' He turned to his warriors, showing his back to Layak. 'Kill him.'

The air churned with animal groans, and the surfaces of the pits boiled as half-formed creatures began pulling themselves from the depths. They were pathetic things, born too early or too quickly. Barely human, their skin split as it tried to cover too much muscle, spears of sharp bone jutting from their joints. Some simply collapsed under their own weight before they could lend their strength to the defence of the mountain, their bodies rupturing and spilling foul fluids back into the pits from whence they were birthed.

Barnhart quickly learned to conserve her shots, not wasting the valuable energy on such abominations, saving them for more pressing threats. There were many. They crawled from the pits alongside their cursed brethren, larger even than the Space Marines, and maddening in aspect. They were human only in so much as they sported skin and hair the same as her own. In almost every other sense, they were monsters – amalgams of meat and bone with too many limbs, too many eyes, like a dozen bodies had been folded desperately together to form golems of flesh.

She fired to an internal rhythm, trusting her shots to the silent prayer she counted. She had been taught to aim for the head, but these creatures of nightmare didn't seem to have heads, or at least, not just one.

Her squad chose their own targets. To a person they were exhausted, and the injuries they carried would have felled lesser men and women. Their minds were reeling, just as Barnhart's was, from the inexplicable things they had seen on this world, but they remained fearsome soldiers, hardened by a lifetime on the battlefield. She felt a fierce pride as they held their defensive perimeter, unwavering even as the golems came close enough to smell the sulphurous stink of their skin.

'Hold formation!' she called, as much to herself as to her squad. 'Maintain contact with Lord Layak, we are to get him that blade.'

'They're getting closer,' Palgen said, barely controlled panic in her voice. 'Lieutenant, behind–'

The sentence was stopped short as Palgen's upper body exploded. The bolt shell had hit her square in the sternum, the impact of the mass-reactive explosion sending what remained of her skull arcing high into the air, while her lower body slumped to the fluid-slick ground below. In death, she had saved Barnhart's life – she had turned at the warning, ducking the swing of a bone blade that would otherwise have removed her own head from her shoulders. She threw herself backwards, cursing, and brought her lasgun up, firing from the hip at the shape that had swung the blade. Las bolts lanced into its central mass, a clump of twisting fat and muscle surrounding a leering, half-formed face. Rheumy eyes fizzled and burst, the projectiles burning away the outer layers of muscle fibre to show yet more pulsating matter beneath. The creature kept coming. Barnhart checked her power pack – a third left. She fired two more shots into the beast, and made a decision. Layak had been swarmed by the mutants, their assault renewed as their master called for the Space Marine's death. She would reach him, or she would die trying.

Layak was used to fighting alone. The Ashen Circle specialised in such combat, deploying in small groups and breaking off to burn centres of culture, execute firebrand preachers, and otherwise break an enemy's morale. Alone, he had killed hundreds, thousands – but by and large they had been librarians and acolytes, cultists and thralls. These mutants, slow-witted though they were, fought with the strength of Legion brothers. Some of them had the weaponry as well. Bolt shells clanged from Layak's armour, defacing the holy script that had been etched onto its ceramite surface, and it was all he could do to keep moving through the throng, not letting his attackers sight a killing shot.

But Layak was no ordinary Legion brother. He understood the principles of fleshcraft – had dabbled in it himself – as well as many other, more advanced sorceries.

The rituals of soul binding usually took longer to prepare, but Layak kept the tools about his person, just in case. Charms and relics, vials and bones – objects of power that could be used in the process. He prepared them as carefully as he could, pulling them from pouches and containers. Of course, they were useless without a catalyst, but he had one in abundance.

Pain. Pain was the engine to drive the change. He pulled flame from the foetid air and sprayed it across the closest mutants. They squealed and gibbered as it chewed through their malformed muscles, and he siphoned off some of their agony to cut a rent in reality. Iridescent shapes crawled through – beings with lash-like tails, poison-dripping pincers, and long, searching tongues.

The mutants were simple creatures, and they panicked as the Neverborn cavorted amongst them. Layak took his chance, chanting the words, and exerting his will on the weakest of the herd. Their psychic defences were non-existent, and he forced his way into their heads with ease.

The closest mutant turned to regard him, its piggy eyes blinking slowly. It was a pathetic being, broken from its tortured birth, but he felt its dull urge to fight, to kill, to grind and eat its foe's flesh. And so, he ordered it to sate itself of all its desires, and watched as it turned, swinging a humungous fist into the face of one of its cousins. The first blow detached the second mutant's jaw, and the second removed it entirely. Entranced by the sight and smell of blood, the first mutant grabbed the second's head and wrenched it from its shoulders, squeezing it so hard that the skull burst open, showering red-and-grey matter across the chamber floor. The mutant bounded off, already looking for the next thing to kill.

Layak used the mutants as cover, binding more and more, until he had built his own cadre of soul-bound creatures. They battered and broke their brothers, pulling them apart as they rose from the bubbling pits, loose skin tearing and swollen muscles ripping – violence beyond measure – until the chamber's sandy floor ran red with their blood. Hebek and Kulnar lumbered amongst them, hacking and cutting with their Anakatis blades, steadfast even as bolter shells blew chunks of ceramite from their armour and gobbets of meat from their bodies.

Saucan's satisfaction had soured, and the Chapter Master

scowled from atop the dais, his vaunted army unable to land a blow on his brother.

'This is your new Legion,' Layak called, using sorcery to project his voice. It echoed from the ceiling high above, sending the strange flying creatures shrieking between their stalactite homes. 'Pathetic. They are abominations. Lorgar will kill you himself for the shame of their creation.'

'Kill him!' Saucan roared, and as Layak took the mind of another mutant, the Chapter Master tore the bolter from the grasp of his closest bodyguard. He launched volleys of bolt shells from the muzzle, firing fully automatic, trying to find Layak amongst the mass of half-formed flesh. Mutants juddered and died, shrapnel and fire shredding and scorching their twisted forms.

Saucan howled, and hurled the bolter from the dais. 'Stop!' he called, loud enough that he could be heard over the din.

His mutants did as ordered, and Layak followed suit, standing amidst his soul-bound mutants, panting heavily. Hebek and Kulnar, previously metronomic in their killing, had ceased fighting entirely, their blades held at their sides and their heads low, in apparent deference to Saucan's blade.

'Enough. Some vestige of honour must remain in your tattered soul. Let us settle this as warriors,' the Chapter Master said.

He shrugged off his cloak of flesh, letting it fall from his shoulders. Stunted humanoids rushed in to collect it, folding it quickly between them, and lolloping back into the gloom. Saucan shouldered the Anakatis blade, and beckoned Layak to the dais.

Lorgar stood behind him, invisible to all but Layak.

'It is time,' the primarch said.

Layak stepped forward. 'I accept.'

'You will die here,' Saucan said.

'I know,' he said.

CHAPTER TEN

The dais was natural in construction, the aeons of sediment laid down in a pattern that offered a commanding view of the whole chamber. Its surface was covered in loose sand, like a gladiator's pit, and Zardu Layak's boots left impressions in it when he stepped up to join his brother.

Saucan pointed the tip of his Anakatis blade into the loose sand, and drew three slashes there. The symbol of the gate – of his Chapter.

Layak drew no symbols in the dirt. His symbols had already been inscribed into his armour and his skin, symbols of warding and of dedication. The future of the Legion, writ into his own flesh. He readied his axe-rake, holding the weapon loose in his right hand, his finger light against the trigger. He held his left hand open, palm exposed towards his opponent.

'Come, then,' Saucan said.

'Before this ends, I want to thank you, brother,' Layak said.

'For what?' Saucan spat. He pulled the blade from the floor, using the momentum to describe a full arc around his head.

'For finding the blades. I am glad you could fulfil the task I set you.'

'You did no such thing.'

Layak smiled, showing his teeth. 'I sent you here to find these weapons – you, Hebek, and Kulnar. I chose you, as my closest brothers, to help complete my sacred duty.'

Saucan scoffed, as if waiting for a punchline. It did not come, and realisation dawned.

'Gods, you truly believe that? That we were fulfilling a purpose on this forgotten world?' Saucan laughed. 'You are mad, boy. You were already broken when I allowed you into the Chapter, but this is beyond what I could have imagined.'

'I saw the blades in a vision, and sent you here...'

Saucan cut him off, incredulous. 'You? *You?* You did not know about the blades. I found them!' He levelled the weapon at Layak's face, and its bloodshot eyes met his own. 'It was I who led my brothers into the mountain, I claimed them from this altar, I used their power to build this place.' Saucan emphasised each point with a swing of the blade. 'You banished us here! You came on us in the darkness, with blood sorcery, rendering us insensate. You brought us to this place, and left us – cut off from our Legion, from our war.'

'No,' Layak said, voice faltering ever so slightly. 'I–'

'You knew that each of us stood in your way. A braver man would have killed us all, but you were too craven. You have always been too craven, hiding behind prophecies and visions, never able to take responsibility for your choices.'

Pain filled Layak's skull, and he threw a hand to his forehead. 'I sent you here, I know I did. I remember it.'

Darkness spilled from the ochre gate, slowly eclipsing his thoughts. He stood with his brothers...

No.

He stood alone. Three bodies lay at his feet, ensconced in coffin-like apparatuses with transparent upper halves. They beeped occasionally, the life signs of the things inside nominal.

'You sent them here,' Lorgar said. 'You have tried this many times before, have been ready to take the next step many times before. But you always faltered.'

'You have built a truth that is mere convenience, a web of lies and half-truths spun to support a diseased mind,' Saucan said. Red power armour whirred as he stepped forward, Anakatis blade an arm's reach from Layak's throat. Layak smashed the blade aside with the flat of his axe-rake – a clumsy parry that turned into a guard.

'You are not chosen,' Saucan spat, wheeling to face Layak, blade held in two hands like a greatsword. 'You are mad.'

Lorgar's voice was harsh, a parent chastising his child. 'These three – you knew what they meant to you. You could not kill them. So you used your sorceries, cut their ties to the Legion, severed their memories in the minds of others, and hid them away.'

Saucan stepped forward, shaping to pull the blade overhand, but checked his motion and aimed a kick at Layak's chest instead, embedding the weapon's tip into the dirt floor and using it as leverage. Layak was launched backwards, hitting the ground hard. He tasted blood in his mouth – copper, and sulphur.

'A place where they would not be found. Where they would be safe – where you would not need to take the next step. And then you killed your own memories of the act, so you would never have to face them.' Lorgar's anger dwarfed Saucan's. 'But you cannot hide from me. From us.'

The chamber rumbled, a sound like thunder. The voice of the gods.

'You were always weak,' Saucan said. 'I should have killed you when I had the chance.'

Layak looked up into his Chapter Master's face, contorted by rage. He had seen that face a hundred times or more in the practice cages.

Layak coughed, spat the blood. 'Why didn't you?' he asked.

Saucan snarled as he hefted the Anakatis blade to pierce Layak's heart.

'Loyalty,' he said.

Layak rolled as the Anakatis blade came down. The weapon hissed as it slammed into the ground, denied the taste of blood and the texture of flesh.

He brought himself to his feet and dropped back into a defensive stance. Even with Layak's gifts, Saucan was more than a match for his speed and strength. The blade gave him reach, as well as powers Layak had yet to understand. Kulnar and Hebek would turn the tide of this fight, but they stood amongst the monsters, either unwilling or unable to use their own blades against their brother.

Saucan charged, howling curses and arcing the Anakatis blade over his shoulder. Layak caught the sword on his axe-rake once more, bracing his whirring weapon with two hands. The blade's inhuman eyes met his own as he strained under its weight, black pupils dilating as they took him in. Saucan grunted in exertion, and behind the animal sound, Layak heard a susurration in his mind as the blade whispered in a language he could not yet understand.

Fatigue throbbed in his arms. Saucan had always been the strongest of them, but in taking the Anakatis, he had become stronger still. The warp-sharpened edge of the blade drew closer as his Chapter Master lent his weight to the attack, trying to break Layak's guard.

Layak twisted, turning the blade downwards, past him, into the stinking air beyond. Saucan roared in anger, foaming spittle at the corner of his mouth.

'I hated you!' he thundered. 'A mongrel boy from nowhere. What did you know of Colchis? What did you know of the Legion?' He pressed the attack again, thrusting with the blade, lightning fast. The weapon was heavy, but Saucan wielded it as if it was as light as a feather, pirouetting it at the last second to move with Layak's defensive motion. The blade scored a cut across the ceramite of Layak's stomach armour – not enough to cut skin, but the gentle hiss of releasing fluid told Layak that it had been deep enough to expose the cables that lay beneath the ceramite.

Layak circled, keeping to the edge of the dais. He kept his burning eyes on Saucan as he moved, ready to react to his next onslaught. The Chapter Master was breathing hard now, like an animal, hunched shoulders rising and falling with each lungful of air. His horns had stretched, grown longer since the start of their duel. Fresh blood trickled from his scalp, tracing red lines down his snarling face.

Saucan paced, slashing the Anakatis blade at the air. He beat his own forehead with the palm of his off hand between strikes, the heel coming away red with his own blood.

'My god, a deceiver. My Legion, shamed. And you…' He stopped in his pacing, and pointed an accusing finger at Layak. 'Betrayer.'

'My loyalty is to the gods, just as Lorgar's is.'

'Do not speak of Lorgar!'

The roar echoed from the cavern walls high above, and spooked the creatures that lived there. Strange silhouettes flitted out from craggy outcroppings, howling in voices like human children.

The moment of silence that followed was punctuated only by Saucan's ragged breathing.

'He left us as we knelt amidst the ruins of our Legion. He left me, knelt in the depths of shame.'

A crack echoed across the dais, like a bone snapping.

'We will not be shamed again.'

Red ceramite split.

'I will make sure of it.'

Saucan's legs bent backwards with a sickening crunch. Hooves erupted from beneath armour, glistening with blood and black fluid. Rage metastasised in the Chapter Master's body, cells expanding, splitting, growing ever larger, growing new muscle and bone under a surface of undulating skin.

'I have made an army to conquer the galaxy in the Legion's name,' Saucan said, stretching his arms wide across his domain. 'I will lead it to Lorgar, and grind him under its heels.'

'The gods...'

'The gods will bow to us!'

All poise forgotten, Saucan leapt at Layak, Anakatis blade wheeling as he spun on powerful legs. The ancient weapon cut the air with venom, always just a few millimetres from Layak's twisting form, hissing as it begged to bury itself in blood and bone.

Layak's chest thumped, twin hearts pounding, lungs burning, until he could stay ahead of the weapon no longer. The edge of the Anakatis blade found his armoured thigh, then his pauldron, scraping gouges into the ceramite as if it was the sand below. Layak could only block the next strike with his axe-rake, and the next, and the next – a rain of beast-strong blows that battered against his weapon.

Gods, I beseech you, he thought, as a new future suddenly unravelled in his mind. *Lend me your strength.*

Silence was his response.

Muttering softly, he offered words of warding and of change, but was interrupted as Saucan sent a wide blade strike that would have severed his left arm at the wrist. He tried to meet it with his axe-rake, but realised too late it was a feint, designed to bring Saucan in close. The Chapter Master punched upwards with the hilt of the Anakatis blade, catching Layak squarely in the mouth as he spoke, breaking sharpened teeth and filling his mouth with hot blood.

I am your Apostle, he pressed. *I am Zardu Layak. I am chosen.*

Layak staggered backwards, and Saucan was on him again, swinging the blade as a headsman's axe. Layak threw his axe-rake into a desperation block, and the weapon howled as the blade caught on it. Chain teeth ground into warp-forged metal, and for a moment, it seemed that neither would give ground, until finally, one triumphed.

The axe-rake detonated under the pressure. Promethium erupted from the body of the weapon as the chain belt disconnected from the mechanisms beneath its plated surface. Monomolecular teeth launched high into the air, where they glittered, snowflakes caught in an updraught, before falling back to the ground with a sound like broken glass.

Layak stood on the dais, unarmed.

Please. I am chosen.

A predatory smile split Saucan's blood-soaked face. 'Remember what I taught you, brother? No fight is truly fair.'

I am chosen.

Am I chosen?

The Anakatis blade pierced Layak's gut. It parted skin as easily as it had cut ceramite, but it felt as if muscle was being torn apart, fibre by fibre. The weapon dealt in perfect agony, scorching nerve endings as it travelled deeper into the soft meat of his organs.

Layak opened his mouth to speak, but only blood came to his lips.

He put his hands against the blade. It was cold – as cold as the void against armaglass. He could feel it inside him, ecstasy amidst the agony, drinking his blood, drinking his pain.

'You are weak,' Saucan snorted. 'Your path ends here.'

'It... cannot,' Layak said. His burning sight began to narrow, the flames at the edge of his vision guttering. The path narrowed, the future – the only future – growing cloudy.

I am forsaken.

'Oh, but it can.' Saucan pushed the blade in, deeper still. Layak heard its edge scrape against the bone of his ribs. 'But it does not have to.'

'What do you mean?'

'There is still a way back,' Saucan breathed. 'A way for all of us. To right the wrongs of Monarchia, to bring our Legion from the ashes.' He grabbed Layak's face in his massive hand, and leant in close. Stinking breath met stinking breath, the smells of sulphur and grave rot together. The blood sheeting Saucan's face shone black in the cavern, his wild eyes the only points of light.

'I have not forgotten the bonds of brotherhood.'

Brother.

Father.

Layak felt the skin of his face tear under his Chapter Master's talons.

'I will present you to Lorgar, and he will see the truth of it. That you are weak. That I' – Saucan beat his chest once, the sound like a sonic boom – 'am strong. The strongest of all.'

The Anakatis blades whispered at the edge of Layak's consciousness. A hiss, like a vox tuned to the wrong channel. A word coagulated in his mind.

Forsaken.

'How...?' Layak asked.

'It is simple,' Saucan said, pulling the Anakatis blade from Layak's stomach and pointing it at his throat. 'Kneel.'

* * *

Layak stumbled on unsteady feet, wavering, but not yet ready to fall. Blood flowed easily from the wound in his gut, staining his grey armour crimson.

He looked up into Saucan's bloodied face. A crimson giant, standing over him once more. There was no laughter – not this time. He would not run – could not run. He had only one weapon left with which to meet the giant.

'Gods,' he whispered, swaying slightly. Darkness congealed at the edge of his vision. The darkness beyond the gate, pulling him through. 'I give myself to you. Deliver me, for I am yours.'

Saucan's visage began to change. Slowly at first, like the shifting of sand dunes across a generation, but then all at once, the rage dissipated from his face. The blood faded, exposing a shaven head drawn now with script. The horns became a halo, golden, the same colour as the skin, which shone even in the gloom. The mouth was turned not in a snarl, as it had been, but a smile – warm. Paternal.

'I am ready…' Layak whispered.

Lorgar reached for his son's face. His touch was a salve to agony and exhaustion, a bloom of warmth that radiated through Layak's body.

'You are,' the primarch said.

'What would you have me do?'

'What you have always done.' Lorgar's eyes were no longer gold. They were red, wrathful and stern; they were blue and yellow, ever-changing; they were green, milky with ruin; and they were pale purple, beautiful beyond words. 'Have faith.'

As the words were spoken, Lorgar's face faded, and Saucan stood once more before Layak.

'Kneel!' he roared again, pushing the tip of the Anakatis blade against the skin of Layak's throat.

Faith.

The word echoed in the cavern, and in Layak's mind. So simple. So perfect. So true.

Zardu Layak knelt.

Faith.

'Good,' Saucan said, keeping the blade against bare skin. 'The other blades. They are mine. You will give them to me.'

Faith.

'Yes, my lord,' Layak said.

'You finally see the truth,' Saucan told him, triumph creeping into his voice. 'Father knew it before, and Guilliman hated him for it. The primarch of the Thirteenth hides behind his morals, but it is power that breeds loyalty, not any innate honour in the souls of men.'

Saucan pulled the blade away, raising it high to the roof above, guiding the attention of the cavern's mutants with the weapon as a conductor wields their baton. He turned his back on Layak, facing his fleshcrafted army.

'I have power, and so I have loyalty' – Saucan spun on bestial legs, fixing Layak with a blood-soaked grin – 'even from such a madman.'

Faith, the cavern echoed.

Saucan moved once more to Layak's side, covering the gap in two massive strides.

'And now,' he said, taking pleasure in his victory, 'it is time for your path to end.'

The darkness at the edge of Layak's vision swelled. The future, once unshakeable, immovable, faded from view.

'You said you would spare me,' he said.

'No, brother.' Saucan leant in close, the copper stink of blood filling Layak's nostrils. 'I said I would bring you to our father. And I will.' He laid the Anakatis blade against Layak's shoulder, its edge against the nape of his neck once more. 'As a slave of the blades.'

The Anakatis' whispers were loud in his ear, and Layak could almost make out their meaning, half-formed words in a language still maddeningly beyond reach. The world was a pinprick of colour, as if viewed from the end of a corridor, or through the wrong end of a monocular.

Saucan continued.

'Your betrayal cannot be forgiven. Only the loyal can erase our shame. Only the loyal will be welcomed back to the Legion.'

Layak was not listening. Lorgar stood across the dais.

'Speak the word, and be cleansed.'

'You will not be remembered,' Saucan said, lifting the blade high.

Barnhart was the last one left.

Vilka had almost made it to the outcropping, but her legs had been taken out from under her as she ran, tripped by a golem of contorted bodies double her size. The thing had crushed her head with slab fists, and what remained of her lay on the cavern floor, quietly oozing.

The stone was warm against Barnhart's back. She allowed herself to slide down it, the fabric of her fatigues rubbing against ancient rock, until she was seated on the floor.

She checked her lasgun's ammo counter one more time. It was habit; she knew the answer already.

Enough power for one shot.

She had always wondered where she would die.

Now she knew.

There was comfort in knowing. This was where she had been destined to die. Not in the rad-deserts of Igno IV, or even the bogs of Koifaul, but here, under the mountain. Layak had made her believe again, and there was peace in faith.

She placed the muzzle of her lasgun against her chin.

At least it would be quick.

'I'm sorry,' she said to the ghost of her father. 'I'm sorry for leaving you. I'm sorry for what I became. I'm sorry for everything.'

She closed her eyes.

She felt a hand on her shoulder – a touch of gentleness, incongruous amidst so much pain – and opened her eyes once more.

Her father stood over her. He was as she remembered him on the night of the argument. The night that she had made up her mind. His bald head glinted like the polished buttons of his uniform in the low light of the cavern.

A tear rolled down her cheek.

'But you're...' she whispered. 'How are you...?'

He knelt before her, wiped away the tear with his thumb, and cradled her head in his hands, as he had when she was a youth. His eyes were golden in the darkness.

'Hush now, child. You are exactly where you need to be.'

'What do you mean?' she asked. 'This is the end.'

'No,' he said. 'This is just another step along the path. And you have a part to play.'

He raised an arm, pointing beyond the outcropping, back towards the centre of the cavern. She dared a glance around the corner. Atop the dais, Layak knelt in supplication before the larger warrior. Standing on beast legs, Saucan was every bit as monstrous as his children – a king of blood, crowned with bone. He raised the blade, an executioner's cut.

'What can I do against such power?' she asked. 'I am only one woman.'

Her father scoffed, as he had so many years ago. 'Look how far you have come. Half a galaxy away from your home, leading your people.'

'They died.'

'They brought you here. Their belief brought you here. Belief in you.' He leant forward, put his forehead against hers. It was solid, the skin warm. She saw a world of colour and light inside his eyes.

'It is your calling,' he said.

'I only have one shot.'

He pulled back, standing once more. Gently, he prised the lasgun from her grip, handing it back to her stock-first.

'I believe in you,' he said.

She took a breath, and offered a prayer. The old habit came easy to her.

'I have all I need,' she said, only to herself.

She heard a voice in her ear. Her father, or something else – she did not know.

Have faith.

She fired.

The las bolt streaked the length of the chamber, over the heads of mutants who had never seen the stars, watched over by beings who dwelt among them. A beam of light, of energy, of the matter of the universe, covering the distance in a fraction of a nanosecond. It met its end, finally, where it was always destined to meet its end.

The gods smiled.

Saucan hissed as the bolt hit his wrist. The Anakatis blade felt the pain, too, recoiling from the burning heat, its palpating bone tentacle slipping from around its wielder's arm. Saucan dropped the blade, and it fell to the stone below.

Faith.

Layak took the word up like a weapon. A mantra, first, under his breath, then louder, as a chant, before it became a roar. Spoken in the language of the blades, the words were poison to mortal lips, and they split his flesh as he uttered them. Tongue and teeth, jaw and lips began to tear open, their bones, muscles, skin, and blood vessels rupturing. Still the chant came, through rivers of blood.

'Faith, faith, faith.'

The blade squirmed on the floor, as if rendered ecstatic by the sound. Saucan bent to pick it up, and it skittered from his grip, not wanting to be taken.

Bone cracked and crunched as it re-formed in Layak's mouth, building a new jaw, wide and powerful. Teeth sprouted from sockets, long, sharp, and serrated. Meat grew around this new mouth, lips drawn tight, muscles swollen and warp-strong.

Layak felt the change in his gut, too. The ragged wound closed slowly, skin knitting itself together. Beneath the surface of the skin, failing organs recovered, broken bone regrowing in a matter of seconds. The darkness at the edge of his vision faded, replaced by the burning vitality of his new vision.

Zardu Layak knelt before his brother, remade. Belief's reward, writ large on his body. The boons of the gods.

'Faith,' Layak said, through a daemon's maw.

Saucan looked up from the blade, just as Layak leapt for him.

He clamped his jaws around Saucan's head, and bit deep, tasting blood and agony. They fell to the ground together, and – before Saucan could reach for the Anakatis blade – Zardu Layak began eating his brother's face.

Layak devoured Saucan's flesh like a famished animal, tearing skin and muscle with great rending bites. Saucan's nose lost its grip on his skull and came away in Layak's mouth, its texture rubbery; an eyeball burst between his teeth, its jellied innards spilling down his chin. When screams rose from deep within Saucan's lungs, Layak devoured those too, his brother's pain every bit as sweet as his blood. He only slowed his assault when his teeth began to scrape against naught but skull bone, no longer rewarding him with morsels of flesh.

Still straddling his twitching body, Layak placed a hand on his Chapter Master's armoured collar and lifted Saucan from the ground, bringing his face close to regard his work. He stared into ruin. A single eyeball stared back.

Layak purred in delight, and stood, letting Saucan's torso fall hard. Blood gouted from his open throat, his life steadily draining out onto the rock floor.

'I see it now,' Zardu Layak said. 'I see it all. How this ends, how it all ends. The blades do not open the way. They only brought me to this place. They brought me to you. I was weak, brother – you were right. Where I was going, I could not take you with me. Nor could I take my saviour, nor my mentor.' He gestured to Kulnar and Hebek, who still stood motionless. 'My loyalty. My doubt. My mercy. I was not yet ready to destroy them. I had not understood the truth of it.'

Saucan writhed in pain, curling as he lay on his side, his hands covering his ruined face.

'And so I hid them in my soul,' Layak went on. 'I hid you here on this world, and hoped that would be enough. But it was not enough for the gods. I have been chosen, Saucan. Every cog, every wheel, has turned to bring me to this point. You are blessed, to help me on this path.'

Layak put a boot into Saucan's ribs, turned him over to gaze once more upon his face. The white of skull showed through the red as the Chapter Master's jaw worked in a scream.

'You suffer now, Saucan. I can see it, coming off you like smoke from a censer. Ripe and pungent. It is an offering to the gods. But it is a fraction of the suffering that I have endured, that I will endure.'

The Anakatis blade audibly vibrated, its length clanging against the stone, energised in the presence of such agony. Layak walked the dais like a preacher, speaking as much to the stunned audience as the mutilated Saucan.

'You rage against your shame, against your pain. You fight it, desperate to claw a way back to a time before, when things were ordered. But there is no way back. Chaos is inevitable.'

Saucan tried to speak with half a tongue and a broken jaw. Layak ignored him.

'I know your pain, Saucan. I feel it too. But I have embraced it. Made it part of me. Humanity was born to suffer. Our species rages against our destiny, but it is futile. All of this is written, all of this will come to pass.'

Layak crouched next to Saucan, raised a finger to what remained of his cheek. He traced it down the raw meat of the Chapter Master's face, a gesture of warped tenderness.

'You call me mad, brother. But I am sane. I am the only one with enough sanity to see what is coming. I have made myself ready for it.'

Saucan spluttered something from a lipless mouth.

'What was that?' Layak asked, leaning closer.

'Kill... me...' Saucan managed.

With Saucan separated from the Anakatis blade, Hebek and Kulnar had returned to Layak's control, and he directed them with a thought to heft their Chapter Master's body onto the stone altar at the centre of the dais. Saucan barely struggled, his body well on the way to death by blood loss.

Layak stood at the head of the altar, holding his brother's head with one hand. He closed his bare hand around the blade's haft. It was cold in his grip, and it sang its temptations, promising him power and strength if only he would take it, use it, give himself to it. He was beyond such base offers now. So little of his humanity remained – just one final thread to cut, and he would finally be complete.

He lifted the blade, raised it to the heavens above, and the gods who dwelled within them.

'Behold!' he called, loud enough that his voice echoed back to him from the cavern walls. Loud enough, he hoped, that the gods themselves would hear. 'An offering, in the old ways. Gods of Ruin, see me. I am your vessel.'

He raised the blade, but did not bring it down on what remained of Saucan's throat. Instead, he took his Chapter Master's hands, limp as they were, and folded the fingers around the hilt's grip, allowing the blade's point to rest against his armoured chest. Wordlessly, Hebek and Kulnar stepped forward, supporting Saucan's arms, keeping the blade from sliding into the cavity of his torso.

Layak leaned in close, whispering into the hole where Saucan's ear had been.

'You were right, brother,' he said. 'The man you knew will die today.'

He stepped back, and raised his head to the darkness above. 'With this sacrifice, I am cleansed.'

ABOUT THE AUTHOR

Rich McCormick is a writer and videogame producer whose love affair with the worlds of Warhammer began when he was handed a small plastic ork at a very tender age. He used to live in Japan, but now lives in Yorkshire, with his wife and son. His work for Black Library includes the Warhammer 40,000 novel *Renegades: Lord of Excess* and the short stories 'Knife Flight' and 'A More Perfect Union', as well as the Horus Heresy short story 'Visage'.

An extract from
Ashes of the Imperium
by Chris Wraight

The error of history is to assume greater awareness of circumstances at the time than ever existed; to imagine those of the past knew precisely and with insight what was the case then, what was about to be the case, and what they must do to bring about their desired outcome. So it must be with those days, the days I have made my own study. Will the age come to have its own marker, as the Age of Heresy now has? Will the period become a byword for some particular human failing or accomplishment? Surely it will. And yet, even now, so long after the ashes have cooled, I do not know what it shall be. I propose this, with caution: the Age of Confusion. Or maybe, the Age of Ignorance. For it was this way; there was no certainty, and no ready means of discovering it. As a gravely wounded Terra emerged from its seven-year trial into the fog of a new era, be sure of this one truth: nobody, not a soul, from the greatest of generals to the humblest of soldiers, had the faintest idea what to do next.

– Diomedon of Luna, *A Study of the Reconstruction*

Now run. Run hard. Nothing else exists. Run, then run some more. You will be doing it forever now.

Those were the words, in the rare moments of clarity, the brief pauses in the headlong rush for doubtful sanctuary. It seemed that this was just the start, the movement into a new way of life that would become eternal. Was death preferable? Maybe another fighter would have thought so. They might have turned, weapons held wide, bracing in defiance before the crash of fury-surf that would dash them away.

But he was not made that way. None of his Legion had been made that way. Iron within, iron without. Live. Survive. Fall back, regroup, rebuild. No pity – not for self, not for any living thing. Run. Run hard. Find a place, a distant place, where you can turn at last, and do so from strength.

A place will be found. It will. That was the other truth: the wheel shall turn. Only live long enough to see it.

So run. Run now. But no, not forever.

He had once had a reputation. The earth itself moulded and turned under his hands, they had said. He would gaze at a landscape, a terrain, a scarp that rose and fell like a drape of cloth, and know how to bend it to his will. He would gauge the substrates, the underlying strata and the surface conditions, his grey eyes glittering while his body was held perfectly still under the glow of massed augur readings.

After a minute, or an hour, or days – however long it took – the orders would come. He would signal for the machines to roll into their positions. The drills would start up, the shafts would be delved, the courses dug out. Pumps would begin to churn, soundings would be made. As he continued to observe, arms folded across his chest now, patient, still silent, the levies of slave labour would march into position, tools at the ready. The earth would be changed. It would protest – the screams and bellows of upended stone, the crack of ancient sediments being wrenched into the open – but his will was the mightier. Always, the mightier. The earth was his servant; he was its master.

Thus it had been before the great schism, the years in which he had fought under the banner of the Imperium. Thus it had remained after the break, as victory drew ever closer – the turning of fate's thumbscrew, when his Legion threw off its long humiliation and turned its talents upon old tormentors. The tools remained the same throughout. Not for him the doubtful advantages of the daemonic, the sprites and delusions of weaker minds and souls, just the old, familiar instruments, the physical things: the hammers, the machines, the hands, the mortal minds and sinews.

Bitter, they had been called. Resentful, reclusive. Well, there was a reason for that. A host of reasons. And the Emperor, for all his sins, had never forged a weapon without a purpose. You needed to be bitter to do this work. You needed to put your back into it, to channel all that surliness, to direct the force of it into the soil. Because the deep places were bitter too. They were foul and they were deep, the accumulated spoil of a thousand buried lifetimes, all of it stinking, pulling at your boots and dragging at your shoulders. Only the sour-souled endured that. Only a stomach of wormwood could out-spite the earth.

So they twisted and changed the worlds they found. They sunk their fingers into them and made the terrains into stages of death. Sometimes it was defensive – earthworks and palisades against which armies broke like sheets of glass. Sometimes it was offensive – encircling trenches that covered the advance of the Great Machines and suffocated the life out of enemy fortresses. The result, in the end, was the same. Corpses rotting into the mulch, walls slumping into the mud, war engines condemned to slow rust, and the banners of the IV Legion – the Iron Warriors – raised high once again.

It was methodical. It was patient. It had been perfect, so perfectly planned, from start to finish, the product of a mind of hard genius, and one under whom he had been so proud to serve.

The Master of Sieges. That's what they'd called him back then. Ortag Theokon, the Earth-Tormentor. Honoured among a people who only honoured the most strenuous arts, those of the tool and the instrument, the gauge and the theodolite.

What did it mean any more? There would be no building now. No patient remaking of the earth. Only running, headlong, panicked.

The humiliation of it. The raw, unbearable humiliation. That was the worst wound, far worse than any physical flesh-breaking.

Run. Feel the abjectness, the white-hot shame. Run hard.

MORE FROM BLACK LIBRARY

DROPSITE MASSACRE
by John French

The Warmaster has betrayed the Emperor. Vengeance comes for Horus in the form of seven Legions, but little do the loyalists know there are traitors hidden in their midst.